DESIRES AND ILLUSIONS

DESIRES AND ILLUSIONS

J. Hammerman

Library of Congress Control Number:		2007901416
ISBN:	Hardcover	978-1-4257-5243-9
	Softcover	978-1-4257-5238-5

This book is a work of fiction and solely based on the author's mindset, some situations in this book are based on past experiences while others are not remotely related to any real situation. Any similarities to any person living or deceased, or previous written works is purely coincidental and not intentional.

This book was printed in the United States of America.

To order additional copies of this book, contact:
Xlibris Corporation
1-888-795-4274
www.Xlibris.com
Orders@Xlibris.com

36569

The author would like to add the following acknowledgements.

Thank God for blessing me with the ability to articulate my thoughts on paper.

Thanks to my family for always being there, no matter what situation we encountered. My brothers and sisters who always knew they could depend upon me.

To my mother, although you are not with us physically today I have always felt that you never left. May this book result in the culmination of the success that you always envisioned for me!

Dad, thank you for all of the talks and fatherly advice you have given me, may we continue this wonderful relationship.

My publisher for guiding me through this process and helping an unknown author achieve a lifelong dream, may this book reap us both an abundance of readers and the start of a continued relationship. Thanks to my friends that supported me in this endeavor, especially during the times when I didn't feel I had a chance to get the book published.

Lastly, thank you to those very special people (and collaboration partners) that provided encouragement and inspiration beyond imagination. You have truly redefined the definition of what a friend is and no matter where you are, all of you will always be special friends to me. You know who YOU are!

1 4 3

Foreword

Life can deal us a funny hand sometimes, some days are good while some are just plain treacherous. While we have progressed technology in a lot of areas, the one thing that we have not learned is how to master our feelings for someone. We never know when or where the feeling of admiration will come to us, and most assuredly we usually don't know how to deal with it. Most problems develop when a person talks to their significant other about someone else; jealousy sometimes appears and can lead to an ultimate mess.

This is the problem with Le'Roi, a man who is successful in his business life but his personal life could really use an overhaul. He was a content man with everything in life until he met Jasmine, and that changed everything for him. Sometimes even our best laid plans and desires just seem to find a way of complicating the peaceful skies in our world.

Every decision we make boils down to the choice we made and the consequences that comes with it, be it good or bad. Some roads may look easy, but often time's detours are waiting out of view, and we must make other decisions because of those detours.

It is believed that everyone we meet in our life has a specific purpose, while we may not be sure of what that purpose is, the one thing that is for certain is that we learn something from each of those meetings. Some last only a few moments but leave a lasting impression, while other can last as long as a lifetime. These meetings can either enhance your life or add turmoil to it, as each situation and encounter has to be judged on its own merits.

What will Le'Roi do with the situations he encounters? No matter what decision we make no one really knows how it will turn out; as it seldom turns out the way we really want it to.

OOHHHHHHHH

You've been waiting for me all day long, anticipating my penetration
And you'd like for my tongue to replace your fingers and assist with your masturbation
I got what you need, I'm here to satisfy your desire
I want to taste your creamy torso and use your clitoris as my pacifier
As I begin to slide my tongue in and out of your wet spot, I love the way you moan
The way your body is starting to jerk and squirm, it's really turning me on
So I lift your pussy towards heaven and act like my tongue is in a race
Licking you faster and faster until your orgasm is squirted all over my face
It's dripping off my lips and off the bottom of my chin
Then I throw you down on the bed and go all the way in
Going deeper and deeper until you feel every inch of me inside of you
"That's right girl take it all" is what I'm saying as I slide in and out of you
I know you like it rough so I'm going to give you what you like
I told you I was about satisfying and I'm making tonight your night
So I flip you on your stomach, with your legs spread open, I have you lay flat
Then I go inside you, grab you by the waist with my fingers in the small of your back
As I begin to thrust you can't take it but you don't want me to quit

So I grab you by the head, pull your hair and say "that's a good girl take it"
Now I'm pounding your pussy and you're moaning as loud as you can
Those other dudes only make love to you, now you're being fucked by a real man
And you can't believe this happening, multiple orgasms in one night
You're climaxing while I'm smacking your ass lets me know I'm doing it right
Now you're exhausted all of your strength and energy has vanished
You can't move a muscle, all you can say is "damn that dick is like magic"
I put you to sleep, kiss you on the forehead and tell you that I had fun
Walk out the door, pop my collar, because I know I got the job done

Chapter 1

Le'Roi (pronounced Le-Wah) was born in Chicago; but his family was originally from Louisiana with a distant heritage to France. He wasn't sure how all of that came about or the lineage of his roots, nor did he particularly care, he just knew his name meant something perhaps that was French. While growing up, people seemed fascinated with his name and usually tried to pronounce it as Leroy; children being ever so cruel as they are would always make fun of his name. Adults who should have known better sometimes were even worse; it was only when the family visited Louisiana that his name seemed to be accepted, of course as it was Napoleon who sold the property of the Louisiana Purchase to the United States, I am sure now that a part of him or his Frenchmen wish they had not consummated the deal. While growing up in Chicago Le'Roi and his family were poor and didn't have much of anything, often times he would often have to wear the clothes that belonged to others, but he didn't care, no matter what the condition of the clothes were, they were still like new to him.

His mother worked herself hard trying to provide the best that she could for him, he didn't know what to make of his dad, sometimes he would be there and other times he wouldn't. His mother and father always argued a lot whenever his dad came to visit, he never understood what the argument was about, but he was happy that they were all together. He remembers one day when there was a knock at the door and then momma screaming like she had never done before, he would soon find out that his dad was killed in a car accident.

As the sun rose that morning, there was a mystique that filled the air. Sometimes life can seem so beautiful at times, and at other times just so dreadful. Perhaps things will all work out, then again, sometimes you have to take the cards that are dealt to you and go from there. Inevitably, you either accept things for the way they are or you do something to change it, but what is the correct choice? Sure, everyone can offer advice and tell you what to do, but the ultimate decision lies with you.

Whatever the decision, you alone must live with the consequence of the decision. That's right; you take the good with the bad. Even if what someone has told you makes complete sense, the burden of the responsibility for the choice is never shifted to another and you do what you think is best at that time. The final result of that is to learn from the decision and apply the knowledge gained to future choices. Seems like there never is an easy way out and no matter which way you chose, there was always an alternative, the only question was what cost would be associated with those choices?

Damn he thought; waking up with this stuff on his mind wasn't what he would call a brighter day. There were many days when thoughts like that would wake him from a sound sleep, he didn't understand it, he just knew it happened and he hated the fact that it was beyond his control. He lay in bed and stared at the ceiling, his mind drifting back to his childhood. He remembered how he loved to get up on Saturday mornings and go straight to the television. The cartoons and the cereal made every Saturday seem special, but that was then.

Funny how things change through the years though they remain the same. Things that seemed important back then really have no importance or relevance now. Yes, the priorities have certainly changed as he's gotten older, and wiser. The growing process of changing from a boy to a man seemed transparent to him. In his mind, all he did was make rational decisions while taking other accounts into consideration. His mind seemed to drift back and forth from the past to the present, not wanting to stay focused too long on any one particular event or situation.

For the most part, his life was good and could be called a success, but he never considered himself a success because he didn't want to become too comfortable or complacent. He felt he was somewhat smart, humble and caring. But where does that get you in life? Most people that he has encountered would often try to use and manipulate his kindness for their own advantage. All because he was so trusting, he generally gave people the benefit of the doubt and trusted blindly. The truly remarkable thing is, the difference between his personal life and professional life, they were not even remotely close to being on the same playing field level.

His personal life was in a bit of shambles due to a lack of self confidence and trusting too much, but his professional life was more controlled. Hell, his professional life was very good by all accounts, but when you add the equation of the other aspects, things go downhill from there. He remembered as a child being labeled dumb, stupid, and told he would never amount to anything. Sadly, for the most part, he believed it. He didn't know it then but it would help to shape a lot of his decision making as he grew older, most importantly always trying to win favor in the eyes of others.

Although these things were always said to him, he was determined to prove otherwise but just didn't know how to go about it and prove them wrong. Them was whomever it was that didn't believe in him and put him down, at least he was able to shake that feeling of "woe is me" and not give into the societal labels that often accompany most black men. Yes he was who he was and no one could change that. Judging him from the external appearances, one could say that he felt good about himself and his life. Then again, appearances can be deceiving but as long as you portray the part then it is yours until you give it up. He loved the phrase "Rectal Cranium Inversion". Yes, get your head out of your ass was his motto and it has taken him far to remember that. Then again, that's his professional life.

His personal life was a bit more confusing, fucked up would be the better expression. Shut up he thought, leave that ghetto stuff behind and act like you got some fucking sense. Yep, that's the way his life was. He was a strong black man trying to make it in a white man's world, where nobody gives a damn about you, for you, or for you. Either you run with the wolves and eat the weak or become the weak and get eaten by the wolves. In his professional world he didn't need a pack to run with or someone to validate him, for he was his own man.

Then again, this was the professional side of him and that's what drew women to him, being the trusting person he was made him blind and he didn't always see the true picture. A black man trying to be successful that can express himself in ways most of his peers can't. That was a blessing for him as well as a curse, one he never asked for but nonetheless was saddled with it. What was even more troublesome was the fact that his own ethnic group would often criticize him for being an Uncle Tom, simply because he wanted a better life.

Being a romantic, he loved showering his friends with little gifts, especially the women for they seemed to know him better than the guys, and simply just being different from most other guys made it a bonus for him, it wasn't a competition with anyone more so as it was simply Le'Roi just being himself. Even with the women in his life there were times when he wanted to be passionate and gentle, and then there were times when he basically just wanted to fuck.

It didn't mean that he valued the person any less than what he saw them as, he just wanted to provide for his own pleasure and not always be focused on others. Yes, don't follow society but be your own man was his motto and belief, as he didn't need a special occasion or reason to give something to someone, for it came from his heart and not some societal norm, but subconsciously he did want some things from some people for his own desires.

There goes that part of him that people called Oreo, black on the outside and white on the inside, just like the damn cookie. So many times he tried to fit in and just be normal, but who is to say what is normal. To hell with them he thought, I was born alone and I'll die alone so if it makes me happy then that's what I'll be. Still, it hurt inside that his people usually were the first to attack him for being too white or uppity.

The hurt he felt came from knowing that his own people discriminated against him more than any other race, despite what we have been through. Yet they always talked about the (white) man and how he wouldn't let them be successful. They were too stupid to acknowledge that everything happening around them was mostly due to their own ignorance of understanding how their decisions put them in the predicament. It was always easier to blame someone else rather than face the music by looking into the mirror and seeing where the true problem lies. Even after all these years thinking back on some of his earlier experiences still bothered him.

Realizing he was drifting again, he gathered himself and was back to his thoughts of women and his social life. Yes they loved him all right, or so he thought. Le'Roi loved the women but they were much more in love with the things that they thought he could provide, more so than what they could achieve together. Things would start out so well, his passion would cause him to open up and expose his inner most feelings, making himself vulnerable to attacks from the people he loved. Strangely, he couldn't see it coming; rather, he didn't believe that someone he loved would want to hurt him. He was too trusting, and usually it would come back to haunt him. You can't change who you are he reasoned, it is not my fault if people can't appreciate me for who I am. He knew that he was far from being perfect, but knew damn well that he was better than the bottom of the pool.

He wasn't the rough type, even though he came from that background in Chicago. There were times when he would reminisce about his childhood and growing up on the streets, the things he saw and some of the stuff he did. Looking back he realized that he was fortunate, many of his so-called friends or neighbors were dead or in jail. Some of the poor bastards are just broke and content to beg for handouts on the streets because their lazy asses just don't want to work. He smiled, he liked it when he could go back home and feel the relation of being on the streets. The streets gave him something that no person ever could, an education through the school of the hard knock life!

It made him warm knowing that when he walked down the street people recognized him, even if it was for their own different reasons. Some saw a successful brother that mad it out of the hood, while others saw him as an opportunity to get something from him, which was usually money. Girls that didn't generally give him the time of day growing up suddenly wanted to hand the pussy over to him freely, of course he was smart enough to know that nothing is free in this world. He was content to say no ever quickly and easily, that way it left no doubt in anyone's mind what he was about and after, that's right; let them see what they missed out on he thought as a smile crossed his lips. They didn't give a shit about me when I was here so now those bitches want attention. He didn't like to think like that but sometimes the street side of him just took over.

"Fuck this shit!" he said and went to the bathroom to wash his face. The warm water felt good as he took his time putting it on his face. He looked into the mirror and thought about why he was alone, why couldn't he find someone to appreciate him for who he was? That wasn't the case; it was always about what they could get from him and not what could be put into the relationship to make it work. The really sad part is that it took him years to realize that, what a blind fool he was. That's right; the women wanted him not for who he was, but rather where they felt they could be with a man like him. Use him to elevate their stature and lifestyle and have things given to them without the benefit of working hard to achieve it.

Le'Roi thought about the people that were around him when he grew up, and how some tried to influence him to do things that he knew were wrong, but Le'Roi feared his mother more so than anyone else on the street. He would rather face his worse enemy on the street than go home and have to deal with his mother, who seemed to know everything that he was doing, he never understood how she knew but later he came to learn that the neighbors were also keeping an eye on him and reporting back to his mother. It was the old adage that "it takes a village to raise a child" and his village was all around him, even if he didn't know it.

Chapter 2

Le'Roi's life of growing up on the south side of Chicago presented many challenges and obstacles for him, while he didn't fully embrace the street life that surrounded him, there were times when he did succumb to the temptation to be a "bad" boy. Trying to find a good role model in his neighborhood was like finding the pot of gold at the end of the rainbow, you hear about it but you just can't seem to find it.

There was a pattern to the vicious cycle of poverty, women having babies by different men and the men not caring about the children they fathered. Children growing up in this environment saw these things as the norm and therefore didn't see anything wrong with it, which doomed them to repeat the same pattern that engrossed their life. There were people who could get away from that type of situation, but for some reason they were afraid of change. Le'Roi knew that he did not want to live the rest of his life in this environment, where you have to have someone sit at the window when you opened it to get some fresh air or risk someone crawling in and robbing you. This wasn't a problem if you lived on the second floor or higher, which usually meant that a lot of first floor apartments were vacant and hard to rent out.

Drugs and crime engulfed the neighborhood but his mother made sure that he was having none of that, even when he would hang out with his “so called” partners his mother kept a watchful eye on him. Hell to tell the truth, he feared what his mother would do to him more so than any gang member and everybody knew that you didn’t mess with Miss Jackson or her son.

School was the hardest part for Le’Roi; he was labeled as a dumb or slow child and put in the back of the room out of the way of others. Le’Roi was neither of those things; he just needed things explained to him in a way that he could understand nor did the teachers understand that or even attempt to change their presentation. He became so disillusioned that he stopped trying and still was passed along just to be gotten rid of. Still, his mind was one of a curious nature and if someone told him something he had to test the theory so to speak. He remembered once when an elderly man told him that if you burn a snake his legs would come out, wondering if it was true he set out to find out for himself. Of course being in Chicago there aren’t a lot of opportunities to inadvertently come across one except for the two-legged kind, but Louisiana was different, seems like they had more snakes than people.

One day one of his hang with partners named Rico found a snake in the bushes; this wasn’t your normal garter snake which was colored green with a white stripe, this snake had many colors as it was full of yellow, red, and black colors. Someone probably had the snake kept in the house as a pet and it either escaped or was set free by the owner who no longer cared to provide for it. None of this entered his mind or even mattered to Le’Roi, and the thought of danger was a by-product for him as he brought the shovel down on the snake and wounded it pretty badly.

What should we do with it Rico asked?

Let’s burn it, I want to see if his legs would come out.

Why would you do that Rico asked?

Because I was told that if you burn a snake his legs would come out, so let’s see if it is true?

No one said a word as the wounded snake was scooped up with the shovel and taken into the back alley behind Le’Roi’s house; Le’Roi went and got some gasoline that was for the lawnmower and poured it on the snake. The snake started moving furiously and was trying to get away, but was injured so badly that it could only attempt to try and crawl away. Le'Roi then lit a match and dropped it on the gasoline puddle. The snake seemed to stand on its tail as it ferociously tried to get away from the fiery flames that consumed its body, but with all the strength it had its efforts were to no avail. Looking down, Le'Roi was very disappointed to know that he had been lied to, as no legs ever came out of the snake. Although he was only nine years old at the time, he believed what the older people told him and this was the start of his knowledge gaining process of how people will tell you anything, so that if you didn't believe in something, you basically would fall for anything people would tell you.

Later that evening he saw his mother talking to the neighbor across the street, and then she wiped what seemed to be tears from her eyes. Le'Roi was wondering what she was crying about when he saw her turn and start walking towards the house. As soon as she entered the door she asked him about the snake and he told her what he did, show me she said.

They walked around the back into the alley and he pointed to the charred remains of what had been the snake, when suddenly a searing pain was felt on his back. His mother was beating the crap out of him for what he did; between the licks he was receiving, he was trying to make sense of what was going on.

Later he found out that the reason she whipped him was for being stupid and putting himself in danger as the snake could have been poisonous, but more importantly for burning a living creature while still alive. Le'Roi didn't know that when his mother was a child she lost a brother in a house fire and when told about the burning of the snake he figured her emotional state took her back to that moment. He wasn't sure of the details surrounding the fire as no one had ever mentioned it, perhaps she felt guilty, and he didn't know and dared not ask about it. One thing he knew for sure, he was not going to mess with another snake again.

Things went pretty normal for him after that, he listened to what people had to say but wasn't as eager to prove the theory so to speak. As Le'Roi entered high school, he began to notice the girls. Yes, he had seen them before but he really started to notice them, especially their chest. There was something about a woman's breast that always fascinated him and he loved thinking about them.

He remembered the first time he ever got to touch one, he was pinning a flower on the blouse of one of his classmates and the thought of being so close to them made him shake like a leaf on a tree during a windy day. She smiled and thought it was funny, he fumbled with the flower for so long that she got tired and took his hands and placed them on her chest.

Feel better now, she asked?

He didn't know what to say or do, he just knew they felt good and this was with her clothes on, which only fueled the fire within him to know what they felt like with no clothes on.

Eventually he managed to get the flower on and was all smiles for the rest of the day, whenever someone asked him why he was smiling his would always reply, no reason. Nothing ever progressed between him and the classmate, but she left a lasting impression upon him.

The years in high school went off without any significant drama, except for the one time when he was hanging out after school with some friends when a car drove by, it slowed down then pulled off. No one thought anything of it until the same car came around the school again, this time everyone took notice and stopped talking to see what was going on. The car drove off and rounded the corner again, but this time the window was rolled down and shots rang out, everyone was on his own as each tried to dodge the bullets.

Le'Roi was running down the street when he realized that he was not being chased or followed, he wasn't sure where everyone else went nor did he care at that point, then he realized that the car was still in the street at the same spot, he ducked between two cars and got down to keep from being seen. Then he watched in horror when he realized the guys that were in the car had one of his classmates on the ground beating him with baseball bats. The classmate was screaming and begging before one of the bats caught him in the face, Le'Roi wanted to help but in that case all you would do is get yourself killed, so he figured he had better play it cool and decided to stay down between the two cars.

The guy was lying on the ground barely moving when the thugs got back into their car and started driving off. He was glad it was over when suddenly the car stopped and the driver got out and walked over and put two bullets into the chest of his classmate. Le'Roi's heart rate quickened to the point that he thought he was having a heart attack.

The driver calmly walked back to the car and proceeded to drive off, realizing they were headed in his direction he quickly crawled underneath one of the car's and lay still, hoping that no one knew he was there. The street was eerily silent, and as the car drove by Le'Roi was afraid to breathe, thinking they might hear him. The sounds of police sirens filled the air and the car picked up speed to get out of the area. No one had seen anything nor would they be able to give any details to the police, which was the way of the streets and if someone thought you spoke to the police you were dealt with.

Le'Roi made his way to the bus stop and thought about the situation during the bus ride home. Once he arrived he told his mother what happened and she quickly reminded him like she had done so many times before, the people you hang out with are either going to boost you up, or bring you down. You must be selective in who you hang out with and sometimes you may find it is best to be alone. Had Le'Roi not been there, he wouldn't have put himself in a position to be hurt from something he knew nothing about. He couldn't blame anyone but himself because he was the one that made the decision to be at that location during that moment.

The shooting was the talk of the day at school; the word on the street was that Kenny had taken some money and drugs that were discarded during a police pat down. Kenny didn't think that anyone saw him take the bag but eyes are always in the hood, and for the right price you can find out whatever it is you would like to know.

Le'Roi was keen to remember that as that lesson would come to play in his life later, he just didn't know it. His mother always tried to teach him about life and although he listened, he was slow to learn just how relevant those lessons were.

Chapter 3

Looking back on the things that he had been through, Le'Roi knew that if he wanted to provide a better life for himself and his mother, he had to move on to better opportunities. He desperately wanted to go to college but knew that his grades probably weren't even good enough for a Junior college, but he needed to start somewhere. One day he was passing by a Marine recruiting station when he saw a woman that caught his eye, so he went in and spoke with a recruiter. Hell he figured if all the women in the Marine Corp looked that good then that was his way to go.

Unfortunately he got the run around and became disillusioned as the male recruiter would often miss their scheduled appointments, until the Army recruiter started showing interest. Le'Roi signed up against his mother's wishes, it wasn't that he was disobedient; he figured it was high time he stood his own ground to become the man that she was raising him to be. To him it was only four years that could lead to something more promising, but his mother saw it as the government taking her baby to have him killed in a war. Le'Roi tried to reassure her and ease her fears, but he also knew that it was his decision and that was what he was going to do.

Shortly after high school Le'Roi was in the Army and the experience became an eye opener to him, the things they did made no sense to him and each time he questioned why things were being done the way they were, he received punishment. Later he caught on to the game and learned that they only wanted programmed people who did what they were told without any thought processing of why they were doing it.

After graduating from the initial training phases, Le'Roi's first assignment was at a base in Georgia; people called it hell because it was so damn hot and of course' he noticed that snakes seemed to be everywhere. Of course the beating that his mother gave him over burning a snake still resonated in his head, and he made no efforts to hide the fact that he was afraid of snakes. One day during a training exercise he was lying in his sleeping bag when someone threw a snake into his sleeping area. Le'Roi jumped so high that it appeared that he leaped and unzipped the sleeping bag all in one move, a group of white guys were standing around in a huddle outside and were laughing at what they just saw. Although the snake was dead, Le'Roi didn't know that.

Someone said something to the fact of how can a nigger from Chicago be scared of a little snake. The statement caused Le'Roi's fear to turn to anger, he didn't even care who said it, for in his mind they all were guilty and something had to be done about it. Without saying a word he walked over to the fire point and grabbed the pick axe, taking the metal end off he held the handle like a baseball bat and walked over to the biggest guy in the group and cracked the stupid fuck upside his head. The laughter stopped and the atmosphere became quiet, the others then became scared as Le'Roi raised the handle for another swing. Before he could do it someone grabbed him from behind, then all hell broke loose as the street side of Le'Roi came out and he just started fighting for his life.

Eventually he was subdued and when it was all said and done, three people were injured; one from the pick axe handle, one from a cracked tooth courtesy of Le'Roi's right hand, and the last one from a kick in the groin. Le'Roi was placed on restriction pending the outcome of the situation, everyplace he went he had to be escorted like some damn child. In the end he was not charged with anything but did receive a fine and extra duty, his sentence was light because it was deemed that he was provoked and didn't act with any malicious intent.

After that situation no one fucked with him in that way again, he sort of gained respect from that encounter. Deciding that he needed something else to focus his attention on, he stopped by the education center one day and enrolled for evening classes. While he was not good in math, Le'Roi started taking business courses, not because he was the business type, but simply because it had the least amount of math. That's stupid as hell he thought, but it was the path he chose. He wasn't even sure if he would enter the business field, he just needed something to occupy his time and keep his brain thinking.

Le'Roi made sure that he sent money home every month, of course he had his own basic needs but he often worried about his mother. Each time he would call and ask how things were going she would always say good, which was typical of her. She never wanted to pass her problems off to him and he could sense that, but he also was smart enough to realize her voice told him things she didn't have to tell him. He wondered when she would accept the fact and realize that he wasn't a little boy anymore that would hear her crying some nights. Now he was a man and better able to help her, but she wasn't going to change and he knew that. He was determined to take some of the pressure off her because now he could do so, whereas before all he could do was listen.

While the intent of going to evening college classes was to get a degree, Le'Roi found an unexpected surprise; the women in the classes outnumbered the guys two to one. As time went on he found that some of them wanted to become his "study" partner because they thought that he was so smart, he saw it as them wanting him to do the homework assignment and share it with them. This discovery came after one person who wanted to be his study partner would never show for scheduled meetings, but would always ask for the answers the day of class.

One day during the class break Le'Roi returned to his seat and found a note, there was his name of it but no indication of where it came from. Opening the paper he started reading the note which said "I would love to get to know the feel of your body next to mine, and put my mouth all over you".

Shocked and surprise were the emotions that Le'Roi was feeling, his eyes slowly canvassing the room to try and figure out who wrote the note, but he couldn't get an answer just by looking. He was never really the ladies kind of man and picking up chicks at the club just didn't appeal to him, in his mind all they were looking for was somebody to fuck and pay their rent. Not sure what to make of it, Le'Roi tried to focus his mind back on the class session, but that was easier said than done. After class he waited to see if someone would make mention or a reference to the note, but no one did.

When he arrived back at his place thoughts of the note were heavily on his mind, he pulled it from his pocket and read it several times more before finally putting it down. During the next class session the same thing happened, this time it wasn't a note but what appeared to be a letter, not wanting to be distracted he put it away with the intention of reading it when he got home. Of course the curiosity of who put the note and letter on his desk intensified his curiosity even more.

Feeling tired from work and attending school almost every night, Le'Roi sat down and drifted off to sleep on the couch, forgetting all about the letter and any schoolwork that had to be done. The next day he was on his way to work when he saw the letter on the table and took it with him, during his lunch break he sat in his car and started reading it:

I walk into your place with the only sound you hear are from my shoes as they click against the tiled floor, silence occurs only when I step on the carpet into your bedroom. I close the door behind me and the room becomes very dark, it surrounds me like a blanket as I am not sure what to expect, the faint scent of incense begins to tickle my nose. I feel you come up behind me, my breath quickens with fear and anticipation. You say nothing as you slide your arms around me; your fingertips gently trace the outline of my breast as they press against my dress. I lean back into you; you kiss my neck as your hands move from my breasts to other parts of my body. You press against me as you squeeze and tease my breasts, making my nipples harden from the excitement.

You slowly turn me around and kiss my cheek as your fingers move to unbutton my dress. Your hands feel warm on my skin as you slowly guide your fingertips between my breasts, teasing them by moving your fingers ever so close to my nipples, but not touching them, neither of us speak as I reached out and unzip your pants. I slide my hand inside and squeeze your cock through your shorts; you slowly roll my nipples between your thumbs and forefingers, while moaning softly as I feel your cock growing in my hand.

I gently brush my lips against yours as I remove your hands from my breasts; hold them in mine as I kneel in front on you. You touch my face softly as I reach up and take your cock from your shorts. I lick my lips as I take your cock in my hand and rub it across my lips. I lick the head, my tongue teasing and caressing the tip. I lick under the rim and back to the head. I hear you moan as I take the head of your cock in my mouth and slowly suck it.

My eyes are closed as I slide my tongue up and down the shaft of your cock. I lick you slowly, loving the feel of your skin against my tongue. I lick back to the head and slide my mouth down on your cock' my hands on your ass as your hard cock fills my mouth. You begin to move slowly, putting your hands on my head and pumping your cock into my mouth, I am so excited that I reach between my legs and part my slit with one hand, as I slide my middle finger inside my already wet pussy, my thumb caressing my clit.

I move my finger in and out of my wet pussy, each stroke matching your cock as it slides in and out of my mouth. You push your cock deeper in my mouth, not moving it, as I feel it hit the back of my throat as I suck you. I moan as you take your cock from my mouth, you reach down and help me to my feet. You slide your finger over my clit; I catch my breath as your mouth comes over mine. Your tongue explores my mouth as your finger slides along the wetness inside my pussy.

I grip your arms tightly, my pussy wet and throbbing against your warm finger. You insert another finger into me, when I tighten my muscles and grip your fingers, wanting you deeper, as you finger fuck my pussy. My body tenses as my pussy contracts around your fingers, I dig my fingertips into your shoulders, my hot wet pussy milking your fingers as I cum.

You lower me on the floor asking me if I'm ready to feel you inside of me. You stick your fingers in my mouth and I begin to suck them as your other hand is busy fingering my ass. I lay there looking up at you, sucking on your fingertips, you lean forward and I feel the head of your cock opening my pussy lips. You guide it in and I arch my back, pushing my pussy further onto your cock. You fuck me harder and harder until I feel your balls slamming against my ass.

I feel myself cum again and let out a low scream. I caress my nipple with one hand and grab you by the back of your neck with the other, making you bring your cock deeper into me. You press my legs over your shoulders, using your chest to hold them in place, and began to fuck me with no mercy. I can feel the head of your cock in my stomach. It is such a confusing mixture of pain and pleasure, but I want it all. I want you to tear my pussy up, fuck me like I have never imagined. So I take it and I cum over and over . . . .

Reading this made him very horny, again there was no clue or indication of who wrote the letter, but it did cause his dick to swell. His mind was now going crazy trying to figure out who wrote it, the ability to express themselves in that manner made him desire to know who it was even more.

About a week later he still didn't have a clue as to who wrote the note and the letter, as they were leaving class Cynthia came up to him and said "did you like the letter?" Le'Roi was stunned because he never imagined that it was Cynthia. There was nothing wrong with her but she had the body of a model and a gorgeous face, in his eyes she could have had anybody she wanted, but why him he asked himself.

I thought it was very well worded, among other things he said.

Perhaps we can go somewhere and talk about it? That way you can really tell me what you thought about it.

Sure, I was going to get something to eat; you can join me if you like.

Okay, I'll follow you she said.

Any particular choice of what to eat?

No, I can always find something to eat no matter where we go.

Le'Roi was liking this already, a woman who is beautiful and also easy to please. His mind thought back to a vivid memory of one relationship. Things were good and the sex was great. He did the things he felt any man should do for his woman, until she started taking him for granted and things became expected. The worse part was she would brag to her friends about how she didn't have to do anything because whatever she wanted her man would get it for her, because her man took care of her because her pussy was that good. That's right, she had it going on and if he ever stopped she would just withhold the pussy until he got back in line, she had it all figured out.

One thing she failed to realize, bragging to her friends may have made her popular in her own mind, but it also aroused a curiosity in her friends as they were not getting the same treatment from their man. Maybe if they could just get a taste of what was going on and damn if he's doing all of that then perhaps I can get him for myself, some of them thought. This led to the women coming on to him and sometimes it even seemed they were following him.

Then her world crumbled as the power she thought she had over him only existed in her mind. She became complacent and after an argument about sharing responsibilities told him if he didn't do what she wanted, then he wouldn't get any pussy. With a stunned look on his face Le'Roi stared at her in disbelief, the words she uttered struck him like a blow to the chest. The reality of the situation was he felt that she was using him for her own purpose while intentionally not giving back into the relationship.

When she realized what she said she wished she could take it back, but it was too late. His words hit her like a ton of bricks when he replied; "you're not the only woman with a hole in this town!" If you think that I'm with you for that then you may as well leave because I can get a fuck anywhere! Better yet, lose my name, number, and forget you ever even met me. He walked away and never looked back. Most people assumed that because he was young he was naïve, but they didn't realize the streets will make you grow up faster than anything else. He was always taught to look out for himself because no one else ever would, and he was determine not to be anybody's fool.

Chapter 4

After arriving at the restaurant, they ordered and ate their food while talking about a lot of things; strangely the letter was the last topic of discussion. Yes she was attracted to Le'Roi and he was attracted to her, but she was looking for a bit more than what he was willing to give at that time. He could have told her whatever he felt that she wanted to hear just to get the drawers, but that was not his way. He wanted to be truthful and straight forward, she said she understood when he told her how he felt and the fact that he wasn't ready to settle down with anyone just yet. Still, she wanted to be with him and was content to wait for him.

They agreed to remain focused on school as the end of the semester was near and finals were approaching, that's just like Le'Roi, being first about taking care of business then pleasure. After finals they went to dinner and a club for a drink when Cynthia said "is tonight our night?" Feeling relieved that school was over for the moment and the drink relaxing him even more, sure, why not he replied. They finished their drinks and stopped by a local motel, he paid for the room and they went in. He hadn't noticed it but she had another bag with her, as if she knew this night was going to happen.

Never one to rush into things, he turned the television on and told her that he was stepping out for a minute; he was going to get some snacks, drinks, and condoms. He was not trying to get caught up in some baby momma drama shit, besides, he knew what she said about him not wanting to settle down, but did she really mean it. He was content to kick it with her and basically service each other when it was needed, but nothing else.

When he returned he could see that she had already taken a shower and was wearing a black camisole, she looked stunning in it. Now he knew why she had the extra bag with her. He put the items he bought away and placed the condoms on the table next to the bed; she seemed surprised that he did that but didn't say anything.

He went in and showered, unlike her he didn't bring a bag or any extra clothing items; he did buy a toothbrush and toothpaste while at the convenience store. When he finished he stepped into the room wearing a towel and realized that the television was off and the radio was on. The sound of the music seemed just right for the moment, turn out the lights she said, and he willingly obeyed. While he was not a virgin, he wasn't as experienced with the ladies as perhaps he should have been or wanted to be. One thing for sure though was he is a fast learner, so he would learn as they went on.

Climbing into bed he removed the towel that covered his naked torso and tossed it on a chair before moving over to her as they lay on their side, his hands slide ever so softly over her body, while doing this he realized that she was wearing a short top and panties. His hands instinctively went from her legs, then to her stomach and ended up at her breasts, before working their way around to her butt, it was then that he realized she was wearing a thong. The silk like fabric felt good to him, but he was more interested in what was underneath. He enjoyed letting his fingers play with her nipples as he moved his mouth over the fabric, he slid his hand inside the front of her thong when she stopped him. Let's go real slow and enjoy the moment she said. Not sure of what she wanted or meant, he let her take the lead and figured he would follow.

During some of his previous encounters he didn't realize that intimacy was more than just sex or getting a nut off. He had no one to teach him that aspect and that is what seemed to be the problem with most men, they are not taught that there is more to intimacy than just penetration. Being the smart man that he was, he learned from those past experiences and sometimes he just needed to be reminded.

She starts by kissing his forehead, cheeks, and then his lips. He returns the favor as his lips gently touch hers when he feels her tongue part his lips and slowly rub along his. Right now he is throbbing but rolls partially on top of himself to keep her from finding out, but that is only temporary and she moves her body closer to him.

Then he stops and gets out of bed, he walks over to the curtain and cracks it ever so slightly so that a bit of moonlight shines through. Their eyes having adjusted to the dark room being gently lit with moonlight, he is laying on his side as he watches the moonlight provide an image of her body as it glistens off her satiny skin.

He watches with much anticipation as she removes the panties and tosses them to him, he picks them up and sniffs her scent on them. Then he watches as she slowly removes her top, even though the room is dark, he can still see the natural curvatures of her breasts, and he couldn't wait to play with them some more. She walks over to the bed and asks him to sit up and open his legs; she joins him on the bed and does the same thing while she faces him.

She leans back with her legs spread wide, giving him the most perfect seat for the erotic show that is about to begin. Can I turn on the light he asks? No. But it is hard to see because there isn't enough light, and I don't want to get cheated out of seeing your beautiful body. Close the curtain and turn on the bathroom light. He does so and returns back to his position on the bed, there was no way he could have anticipated just how beautiful her body was, looking at her made his somewhat limp dick spring back to life.

Cynthia begins by rubbing her fingers gently over her swollen lips, separating them softy as if to show off the flower within, and massaging the hood of her thick clit, slowing and seductively coaxing it out to be played with. He smiled as he thought about how sensitive a woman's clitoris is and how certain touches can cause some serious orgasms. The sight of her hips slowly beginning to rise and lower in front of him is like seeing erotic art in motion, he loved the way her body moved as she pleasured herself. His hand moved to his manhood as he begins to rub himself.

Her thumb and forefinger relentlessly rub and squeeze her throbbing clit, while she spreads her legs even further open to ensure he is able to watch everything. Knowing that orgasm is imminent, she raise her legs in the air and ever so slowly inserts two fingers into her hungry pussy, moaning softly as the feelings surges through her and her pussy coats her fingers with its thick honey.

As her fingers slip in deeper and pull out further with each movement, the juice slowly oozes out and run down to the crack of her ass. "God, this feels good" she moans, then slowly and artfully begins massaging the inner walls of her secret garden. The aroma of her wet pussy fills the air. The sucking sound of her gripping pussy and her heavy sighs and moans pierces the sounds of the radio in the air, as her fingers continue to penetrate deeply into her wet pussy and come out wetter with each thrust.

The light from the bathroom shines on her thick, honey brown thighs and illuminates the sticky wetness the she rubbed on her thighs and stomach. Le'Roi is now stroking himself as he is consumed with desire, he had never witnessed a scene like this and he was content to enjoy the moment. Her hips move faster and faster while her swollen clit fills with more blood, making it grow larger. Help me cum baby she whispers softly, desperately wanting to feel the orgasm that is about to explode inside of her.

I'm so close that I can feel it, come on and help make me cum. Le'Roi moves towards her and places his hands between her legs, he feels the wetness on her thighs as his hands slide under her round ass and raises her hips effortlessly to his hungry mouth, until only her shoulders and head are on the bed and her legs are locked behind his head. “You are so wet, I can drink it out of you” he whispers, then slowly inserts his tongue into her inviting pussy.

The juice of her honey coats his tongue as he moves it in and out of her soft cavern. Her hips jerk upward as the pleasure overtakes her body and she finally succumbs to the orgasm that is swiftly coursing through every pore of her body. He moves his tongue from her hole and firmly locks his mouth on her clit and gently sucks it like a straw, while flicking his tongue across the top, causing her to scream and thrust her pussy into his face. He watches as her facial expression gives the appearance of her being in pain, but he knows it is all due to her being satisfied and he was intent to do that.

“YYYYYEEEESSSSS” she screams, as the explosive orgasm takes over her body. The juice flows from her precious pussy until her body goes completely limp and that beautiful look of satisfaction and erotic pleasure slowly appears on her lovely face.

Le’Roi moves from her hips to join her at her side, he puts on a condom and places her legs over his hips and slides his member into her wet and inviting hole. He watches her facial expression and sees that her forehead tenses from his tool moving in and out of her. The wet juice makes it easy to glide back and forth into her, while his right hand squeezes her breasts.

Le’Roi makes it a point to vary the rhythm and speed of his strokes just to make sure she is able to achieve another orgasm, he looks at her and realizes that she is close, he sees the same type of facial expressions he saw before, this encourages him to make it happen even more.

Suddenly, she thrusts her hips to meet his strokes as she tries to pull him deeper inside of her. She is going buck wild when she begins to tremble and shake; Le’Roi grabs her body and pulls it close to him as he puts every inch of him deep into that pussy. She has another intense orgasm when Le’Roi comes on top of her and begins the ritual again, she looks at him with seemingly tears in her eyes and says “I love you Le’Roi”. He stops and looks at her with disappointment in his eyes, he pulls himself out of her and gets out of bed, he then heads for the shower without even saying a word.

When he finished showering he enters the room and sits in the chair, what's wrong she asks?

I don't want you to love me, I told you I cannot give you what you are looking for and when you said those words it let me know that you are still hoping for something.

That was said in the heat of passion.

That maybe true but I didn't want to hear those words.

Can we try this again; I won't say it this time.

No Cynthia, I think that it is best that we just remain friends and nothing more. I don't think that you can control your emotions and I am not ready to get involved with anyone

Can we at least just stay the night together, I promise nothing more will happen.

We can't guarantee that and I don't want to make things worse than what they are.

You make it sound like I did something really bad she replied.

To you it may seem insignificant, but to me it's a major deal.

Obviously there is a reason for you feeling this way but I just want to spend the night lying next to you, we can even get dressed if that would make you feel better, yes it would he replied. They each put their night clothes on and lay in bed next to each other. They started out far apart but somehow she ended up next to him and placed her head on his chest. They didn't say a word and the only sounds were from the radio. It may have been his imagination, but he thought he felt tears on his chest when she was lying on it. In a way he felt sorry for her, wanting to be loved so bad that she would go to any lengths to get it.

Why didn't women get it, some guys don't need a piece of ass to be with you. He knew this type of thinking was the exception to the rule but he was not about to compromise what he believed just to appease someone else. He thought he was in control of everything as he had been thus far, little did he know that somewhere in the future that thinking would be put to a major test. While his mind was going in all different directions, suddenly, a strange feeling came over him and he didn't understand it or knew what it was. He became very anxious and nervous, sort of restless. He chalked it up to the encounter with Cynthia and tried to dismiss it, but he couldn't. Finally he got up and made himself a drink, turned the radio off and the television on, still he was restless. What the hell is going on he asked himself.

Eventually he was able to lie back down and Cynthia moved right up under him just as she had done before. The sight of such a beautiful woman wanting to be loved and willing to go to any lengths to try and get it was such a pity, she deserved better than that, it just wasn't going to be with him.

Later that night he felt her push against his body, his dick became hard and he slowly reached over and rubbed her breast. She starts pushing her butt harder against his body when he turned her over and his mouth went straight to her nipple, moving the fabric out of the way he was surprised at how aroused they had become. After a while they got undressed and had a pure sex session that culminated with him pulling her hair and spanking her ass before shooting his load into the condom while he was still inside her. He lay on top of her until he slipped out, the rest of the night with Cynthia was uneventful and that morning they both had breakfast before he took her back to her place and went home. They were very cordial with one another, Cynthia didn't understand what the big deal was and Le'Roi was determined to not let anyone love him.

When he walked in the door he saw that he had a message on his answering machine, he figured it was his mother and decided to check it later. Right now he wanted a shower and some peace to get his mind in order. About an hour later the phone rang, hello? Le'Roi? Is this Le'Roi? Yes it is, whom may I ask is speaking? This is your aunt Barbara.

Le'Roi immediately knew something was wrong because Aunt Barbara had never called him before. What's going on he asked? Look child, you need to sit down because I have to tell you something, okay? What is it Aunt Barbara? Le'Roi, your momma went home to be with the Lord last night.

Chapter 5

Le'Roi went through a myriad of emotions over the next few months, his best friend was gone and he felt that he truly had no one to depend on except himself. The family sent the Red Cross message and of course Le'Roi made all of the arrangements to bury his mother. The family wanted her buried back in Louisiana, but no one wanted to help contribute to the cause as he put it.

It was amazing how so many people can have ideas and input about how things should be done but when it is time to put up to help cover the cost associated with those ideas they never seem to have any money. Since his mother didn't have any insurance, Le'Roi took out a loan to cover the cost of the funeral. He made all of the arrangements and wrote the obituary, he asked family members to contribute to the obituary but when it became too much of a headache trying to get people to agree on what to say and the format, he went solo on the project. This angered many of the family members but he didn't care, as far as he was concerned when all of this was over it didn't matter if they ever spoke to him again or not.

People wondered what was wrong with him because he hadn't cried like everyone else, the truth being told he did cry, just not in front of anyone. He was always in control of his emotions and no one was going to change that, so while they may have been critical of him he didn't care what they thought. He stayed in Louisiana for a few days after the funeral and burial, he really didn't want to because he didn't know his family and they seem to often criticize rather than praise. He wasn't sure what caused the rift that brought the family to separate and why his mother moved to Chicago when he was a young boy, but you could sense the discord and his presence seemed to make people not want to talk.

Upon returning to the base in Georgia, the first person Le'Roi runs into is Cynthia. They talk about what's been going on and he tells her about his mother, she gives him her number and tells him that if he ever wants to talk she is there for him as a friend. Le'Roi is skeptical but accepts the number anyway.

As the time goes by Le'Roi is still facing the reality that his mother and best friend is no longer here. He often wonders what he could have done to make her life better, he recalled a time when his mother told him that the best gift he could ever give her was to make something of himself and escaping the poverty and suffering he encompassed while growing up. Still, he often wonders what he could have done to make things easier on her. He never expected that someone who seemed so invincible to him would be taken away by a heart attack.

Le'Roi doesn't call Cynthia right away and for the remaining portion of his military contract he strictly keeps to himself, he doesn't even bother to go back to school even though he was so close to getting his associates degree. The day comes when he finally gets out of the military, not sure what to do or where to go; he decides to stay in Georgia and uses his G.I. bill to attend night classes at a college nearby. During the day he works at a local market as a stock clerk and bagger to help make ends meet. He doesn't think about dating, as his mind is purely focused on completing his schooling and earning his degree, because that is what would have made his momma proud. Although she was not with him physically, he knew that spiritually she was always around.

A few months into his self-imposed hiatus, he walks into the classroom and sees Cynthia; he does a double take and sits on the opposite side of the room. He doesn't want to talk to her or anyone else; he just wants to be left alone so that he could focus on his goals. While he didn't want to admit it, he was still grieving the loss of his best friend and really could use someone to talk to, but he didn't want to be saddled with the drama of someone falling in love with him or pretending they understood what he was going through, the last thing he wanted someone to give him was false sympathy. He didn't understand why people couldn't control their emotions as well as he could. After a couple of weeks Cynthia asked a classmate if she could trade places with them so she could sit next to Le'Roi, the deal happened.

I was hoping that you would have called me by now she said one day. Not knowing what to make of the situation, Le'Roi asked Cynthia what her angle was. She explained that she knew he was hurting from the loss of his mother and also that she was merely looking for a study partner as the class was very hard for her, and she knew that he could help her get through it. Reluctantly he agreed. While he wasn't initially receptive to the idea, he actually enjoyed Cynthia as a study partner; she pulled her weight and provided an insight into scenarios that he hadn't considered, as she was the opposite of his thought process, which was good.

As they worked together Le'Roi felt he didn't have to be so cold towards her and started opening himself up. During their discussions he found out that she was also out of the military and doing basically the same thing that he was. They even went out a couple of times but it was not called a date, and each went back to their respective places, Le'Roi remembered what happened the last time they were intimate and even though much time had passed, he was still cautious.

Things were going very well until one day she showed up looking distressed, sensing that something wasn't quite right with her so he asked what was wrong, she confided in him that she couldn't afford an apartment, car payment, credit cards, and to go to school. So Cynthia did what she thought she could do, she asked Le'Roi if she could move in with him, he backed away from her. No, it's not like that. I would pay my share of the rent, utilities, and food; I just need to get myself together for a few months so that I can get back on my feet.

What about your family, can they help you out?

My family and I are not on the best of terms because of some situations that happened. I had a bank account that my family had access to just for emergencies, one day I checked it and it was closed out and all of the money gone. Of course I asked and nobody knew anything, I never got my money back but I also stopped speaking because of that. Some would say that I was stupid for doing that but growing up poor I knew what it was like to struggle, I was only trying to help them out.

I can't say that I know how you feel because I have not been in that type of situation before, and I am not going to judge you for doing that. I don't mind helping you out but we have to set some rules and conditions in order for us to co-exist, he said. I can live with that, I really can she replied.

They set the conditions and Cynthia moved in with Le'Roi. Things were going very well as there was a fine line that was not to be crossed, mixing business and pleasure didn't work well and Le'Roi wanted to remain focused. Although they lived together each was given the respect and privacy to see other people, he went out twice for dinner but that was the extent of his involvement. If she was seeing someone he didn't know it as she never brought anyone back to their place, most likely out of respect for him.

Just like she said, in a few months Cynthia was able to get herself together and was ready to move back out on her own. They had some good times together as well as some arguments that to this day he really didn't know what they were about. Le'Roi didn't want to see her leave but would never admit that to her, he not only enjoyed the financial aspects of their relationship, but also the fact that he wasn't alone. He truly desired someone of her caliber, but the reality of the situation said that everything he wanted was just an illusion.

It was amazing how well they seemed to work well together, such as if either of them saw something that needed to be done it was; it didn't matter who did it last. Cynthia had found a small opening in his heart but didn't know it, as he was determined to maintain his composure.

Right before she moved out, Le'Roi and Cynthia celebrated with a bottle of wine and a fabulous dinner that she cooked. This is my way of thanking you for trusting me enough to let me stay here until I could get back on my feet she said. No problem he replied. They ate and dranked the wine while reflecting back on some moments they shared, and somehow along the way they ended up in each others arms, they made sweet passionate love that night, and it was better than the first time they were together, the feelings he was starting to feel bothered Le'Roi more than he had ever imagined. Still, he said nothing to her about it. What bothered him was the fact that he was starting to have feelings for her, he didn't know why he was afraid for someone to love him. In some odd way it was his defense mechanism that protected his heart, if no one loved him and he didn't love, then he couldn't be hurt he reasoned with himself.

They kept in touch and each continued their schooling until they graduated with their degrees, his in business management and hers in accounting. After that each set out on their own path, not knowing if they would ever see each other again

Le'Roi set out to establish himself as a respected business man, he found an entry level position in a company in Savannah and moved there to begin his new life. He didn't mind starting at the bottom as he was determined to make a mark for himself and go higher. One thing he didn't expect was the political climate of the company, he had to quickly learn the ropes or risk reaching the glass ceiling that was lower than his desired goals.

Each time there was an opening in the company; Le'Roi would measure himself against the requirements for the job and then work on making himself qualified for the position, even if he didn't apply for it. He wanted to make himself marketable so that he could become the person in demand. This included him taking classes online and at night, which eventually earned him his bachelor's in business administration. So while most people were content with being where they were, he was always working to make himself better, and coming to work on time was a big problem for some people. The military was good for keeping him disciplined in that area, but it was his mother's teaching that was the foundation of his values.

Often his mind would think back to the time when he was with Cynthia and wondered what she was doing; he lost her number and thus had no way of contacting her. He thought back to the one time they had an argument because she expected him to read her mind and he figured why the hell can't you just tell me. He smiled at the thought of it and the truth being told, he really did miss her, more so her qualities than anything else.

He remembered the days when he would long to see her, they were good when they lived together but it always seemed that he was blocking her out as if there was something wrong with them coming to love each other. That much she didn't have to say it as he could see it in her eyes, the good thing is that she didn't say it.

Being with her was truly a delight and a privilege in his mind, but the biggest problem was the inability on his part to open up and express what it was he wanted from her and to allow her the opportunity to be a major part of his life. This was equally frustrating to her as she would express herself during heated moments and he would often wonder "where the hell did that come from?" This happened because he was not adept at reading her mind or willing to let her into his heart.

I guess men and women do come from different planets he thought, women have no problems expressing themselves while men seem to think that doing so somehow makes them less of a man. Maybe one day he would see her again, or at least come across someone with the same qualities and attributes that she possessed.

Le'Roi had quickly worked his way up to an assistant manager position and had his eyes set even higher, this caused some animosity because other employees that had been at the company longer felt they should have been given the position. Of course this caused a rumor to surface that he was a kiss ass Uncle Tom. Le'Roi didn't care, people were always trying to get close to him to find his secret for being the self proclaimed "top dog", those silly individuals probably thought it was something he bottled and kept hidden from the world.

They were too stupid to realize it was how you presented yourself and what confidence you displayed that made you stand out. A person unsure of themselves would soon be revealed and the world would know it. Basically it boiled down to this, if you didn't believe in what you were doing it would show, that kind of unnerving would push potential clients away. You had to not only save money, but also do the job better than your competitors. Too simple for him, as any idiot should have been able to figure that out.

Then there were the women in the company, always trying to get close to him as if he was some kind of trophy for someone's display case. There would always be parties or functions where people were trying to match him up with someone, as they assumed he was lonely and needed someone in his life. Le'Roi had his so called "friends" who clearly understood that just because they hooked up sometimes, them being together was nothing more than a relief session for the both of them, he didn't want any drama and thus didn't bring any either.

Little did most people realize that he was more focused and consumed with closing the deals that made him so popular and successful, rather than banging some chick in the sack. There were plenty of women that caught his eye but he had one policy that was to never be broken, he was never the one to shit and eat at the same place so to speak.

His position was strictly business oriented and he was determined to remain focused, this caused him to not really pay close attention to anyone, especially someone in a romantic way. That is what kept him business focused, as he could sign a client to an account with little or no effort, and back up everything he offered to the client while most people could only dream of doing that. That's why he was respected as "The Man".

Chapter 6

One morning he was awaken with thoughts on his mind and immediately realized that he was reflecting back upon his childhood, it caused a lot of mixed emotions to surface and sometimes it seemed that the things he was thinking about were happening right at that very moment; this was usually the norm for him. Le'Roi never understood why his thoughts would suddenly revert back to his childhood or situations that occurred during that time of his life. He could control his emotions, but he hated the fact that he wasn't able to control the thoughts as they would appear sometimes at the most inopportune moments. He was happy when he thought about the good memories of Saturday mornings and the holidays. It gave him a nostalgic feeling that he never wanted to lose, for those were some of the happiest moments of his life that he treasured.

He thought about the pets he had as a child and how close he became to each one, one pet that stood out was the dog Dobie, who was a German shepherd that was picked up as a stray but eventually, became a lifesaver for the family. Dobie protected the house and wouldn't let anyone come in, sometimes even relatives; I guess he knew better than to trust them. It is funny how animals seem to have a keen sense of trust or distrust of people, while humans can't see that for ourselves. Dobie eventually was put to sleep from old age ailments.

He also remembered how hard and tough the streets were, either you joined the game or you were eaten alive. The drugs, shootings, and killings were a common everyday occurrence. You either learned to adapt or you perhaps became the next target. He knew that wasn't the life for him and was determined to leave it behind and never return. That however would become harder than he ever imagined, for the roads of life are filled with treachery, deceit, and foolishness. No matter how mild mannered you may think you are, sometimes you just have to take it back to the streets to get your point across.

Although he presumed himself to be an educated man, there were times when the street hood within him would surface. This was good as it served as a reminder of where he came from and where he was at the present time, such a contrast he thought. He disliked that aspect of his life while growing up, but also found it necessary to bring that side to the front whenever he was confronted or challenged; it was usually when someone felt they could talk to him in any manner they desired. He was not about to take that shit off anybody, especially someone who was born with everything while he had to struggle to get the meager crumbs that were thrown his way.

Times like this he truly didn't understand, why would he repeatedly reflect on his childhood and bring forth the flood of emotions that either made him smile, or emotionally down just thinking about some of the crap he experienced. He reasoned that it was that type of reflection that kept his drive going to keep achieving and not become complacent with a so-called "good life".

Now he was in a new city with a new beginning, things were going well at the job but the childhood thoughts always surfaced, even at the most inopportune moments such as business meetings. It wasn't that he was trying to run away from anything, he just wanted to understand the what, why, and how. Moments like those were when he missed his mother the most, for she could always explain the dreams to him, even if her interpretation wasn't true. He missed her dearly and though time had passed, it was almost as if she was still here with him.

One day after work he was relaxing in the house pondering his next presentation, he was sipping on a drink when he decided to check his email. It was his personal policy to never take work home from the office, and he made sure his private life was his business. Yes both environments were sacred, and he dared not intermix the two, both lines were clearly drawn and never crossed. Merely thinking about something wasn't the same as actually preparing the presentation, so in his mind he didn't break his rule.

Reading his email he came across a message titled "Let's meet", he didn't recognize the email sender and wondered why it didn't go to his spam folder. He was about to delete it when curiosity got the better of him and he opened it, it was surprisingly full of details about places he had been around town and signed by Sabrina. He responded and asked if they had ever met?

While continuing to check his email and just browsing around the Internet he received a response to his question, in it was an invitation to add her to his messenger for a chat session. Now he was really curious as to whom this was and if he really knew her. He started his chat session and added her I.D. to his account and immediately a chat session was started with Sabrina:

Hi she said.

Hi to you he responded. Do I know you?

Sort of, I work at the grocery store where you shop

How did you get my email address?

I did a search for it on the Internet.

How?

I will tell you but you have to promise that you won't get upset.

Now why would I do that?

Because I could lose my job for what I did, and I don't want to get into trouble.

Well that depends on what you did?

Let me turn my webcam on she said, hold a moment.

He wasn't sure if she should do it but he was curious to see who it was and besides, he could see her but she couldn't see him, so he accepted the invitation. It was the light skinned cashier that always spoke to him but he never really paid any attention her, as she seemed a bit young for him and he was focused on his career anyway.

Can you see me now?

Yes I can, and I know who you are now.

Now will you make that promise?

Yeah I guess so, what did you do follow me home?

I got your information off your check and did an email search for you

You know what you did is illegal right?

Yes I do, that's why I asked you to promise. I don't mean to cause you any trouble.

So what is it you want from me?

Nothing I just wanted to meet you and maybe have some fun.

What kind of fun? I am not really a fun type of guy right now.

Hold please

He watched as she got up and walked away from the camera, she was wearing a large t-shirt and nothing underneath; at least it appeared to be that way. He liked the way her ass moved up and down when she walked and wondered why he never paid attention to her before? Maybe it was the alcohol talking but he started feeling the mood of wanting to get some relief. It had been a while since he was with someone and right now he could use a good fucking, either getting it from her or someone else didn't matter to him, he just wanted some relief. When she returned he could see that she wasn't wearing a bra, as her breasts bounced freely when she leaned forward to sit down, making him wonder what they were like.

I'm back

I see, so what's on your mind? Any plans for tonight?

Nothing at all, just sitting here relaxing.

Okay, what is it that you really what? I am not into games and am not looking for any kind of relationship.

Relax, I am not looking for anything either, I just want to have some fun.

What kind of fun?

Do you have a webcam she asked?

No I don't.

Too bad, do you want to see a show?

What kind of show?

Watch this?

She moves the chair back away from the camera and starts rubbing her nipples through her shirt, he is shocked to see her do this but it also causes an emotional stirring in his lions. He can see her nipples are now hard, as they poke the fabric covering them, his manhood starts to rise and strain against the shorts he's wearing. He didn't know why he was so captivated by watching her as this definitely was not his norm, but he was horny and couldn't stop watching her.

After playing with her breasts she removes her t-shirt and he sees that she is wearing some type of underwear, but her titties looked so damn good. The skin looked so smooth and her nipples stood out, making him want to put his mouth on each one while sucking and nibbling them until she made him stop.

Do you like this?

Very much so, he replied.

Do you have any special requests?

Not really, I have never done anything like this before.

Then you are in for a real treat, sit back and enjoy the show.

She then turns around and reveals that she is wearing a thong, that was why her ass bounced up and down when she walked he thought. It was bigger than he liked to see on a woman but hell, she wasn't his so he really didn't care. He did find himself rubbing his manhood and wishing he was there with her to get some relief. Her hands rubbed and slapped her ass cheeks, occasionally pulling them apart giving him a glimpse of what she had to offer.

Then she sits down in a chair and moves closer to the camera so that he has a better view. She begins to rub her pussy with her right hand as her left hand moves the thong to the side. Taking her fingers, she sliding one, then two of them into her wet pussy, moving them in and out of her box before putting them in her mouth to taste the sweet nectar of her fruit. This fills him with even more excitement as he pulls his dick out of his shorts and begins stroking it.

She gets up and places a towel on the chair and removes her thong, sitting back down, she parts her lips with her hands and rubs her clit, causing it to swell from the excitement and attention. He sees her lean over and wonders what's next? She appears with a dildo and licks the head as if it were an ice cream cone, before fully engulfing it in her mouth. Man if that was my dick she was sucking on I'd really give her something to swallow, he thought.

Moving the dildo down below her navel and stopping at her hot box, she slowly and methodically moves it around before inserting it into her pussy. This causes him to stroke himself even more, wanting to continue until the point of ejaculation. He leaned back in his chair and stretched his legs forward until his member stood straight up, and his balls ached to be relieved of the tension that had been held inside them for so long. His hand moved in mechanical rhythm as he watched her slide the dildo in and out of her sopping wet pussy, seemingly going deeper with each insertion. This continued until her finally erupted and sprayed his juice all over himself and the floor, the amazing part was this orgasm was almost as intense as being with someone, he just knew that he liked it and wanted more.

Sabrina continued on with her show until he cut the webcam session off, not knowing if this was something he should have done or perhaps if it was just her way of getting off by being an exhibitionist. Hell he didn't care as he enjoyed the "show" and was willing to do it again.

Maybe he and Sabrina would actually hook up or even just continue as Internet fuck buddies? There was still a lot he didn't know about her and at this point in his life he wasn't in for any trouble, especially from someone whom he didn't even know. Word travels fast in some places and with his push for upper mobility he couldn't afford to be caught up in a scandal, but if Sabrina was the right person then perhaps . . . .

Chapter 7

He met her on line a couple of times after that and she gave him the usual show, while he really enjoyed watching her play with herself he was beginning to want more than just a watch and jerk-off session. His biggest desire was to know how it felt to be inside that fat and juicy ass of hers, he would do it from behind while playing with her tits, which was his desire with her. Yet all efforts to meet Sabrina never materialized, and he was confused as to why. She didn't respond to his request for a meeting but was more than happy to masturbate on the computer for him. He finally saw Sabrina later at the grocery store, of course that was not the right time or place to say or do anything.

He later found out that this was something she did often; apparently she liked being the art of attention but didn't want the drama of being with someone so this was how she got her kicks, using a dildo on herself while on the Internet. You can find out a lot of things about a person or situation just by sitting in a bar and listening to a bunch of drunken guys talk. He wondered if she knew that she was the talk amongst the guys, hell she probably planned it that way.

This explains why she didn't get upset when he stopped the webcam, there were others watching also while his stupid ass thought that she was simply into him. Yes, it seemed that he was another trophy in someone else's fucking display case and that just didn't sit well with him. Maybe he is looking at this the wrong way, maybe the only thing that some women want is a casual fuck from somebody as long they didn't show any real interest in them. Could it be that he is the one that is out of touch and not them. These were the thoughts in his head and maybe one day he'll figure this shit out.

After awhile it seemed like she didn't even noticed that he existed and definitely didn't seem to care that he wasn't online as much as before, his visits to the grocery store seemed so intrusive that he stopped going and simply did his shopping somewhere else. Nothing was ever said between the two of them but you could feel the tension in the air and he didn't know where it came from, as he had done nothing to harm her. Maybe she had her fun and now found him boring and needed someone new to watch her private shows. He never understood why she did it, but also never got to question why she did the things that she did. Hell not his problem he reasoned.

That was well enough for him as he didn't want a distraction anyway, better to maintain focus and be driven by goals rather than pussy. The company events continued and Le'Roi was poised in a position to be the next head of his department, at 28 he was going to be the youngest department head in company history. This caused excitement and resentment from people in the company, even some of the seniors didn't want this "snot nosed" hot shot thinking he was on their level. Just like everything else, Le'Roi handled it with dignity and class.

During a slow period, a meeting was called to discuss the strategy for an impending project, things were going well and it was then that he saw her. As she was about to take her seat someone spoke to her and he found out her name was Jasmine. He had seen her before but never really took notice of her, until now. Seizing the opportunity he introduced himself and frankly was surprised that she already knew who he was. As they shook hands the softness of her skin felt like butter between his fingers, as the scent of her perfume made her seem that much familiar to him. Funny, it is truly remarkable on how you really can't see the forest if you only look at the trees.

Although he knew that she was with someone else, at least he thought, it didn't stop him from wanting to find out more about her. It was never his point to cause anyone in any kind of a relationship problems, but he wanted to know more about her and the funny thing is he didn't even know why. It has been said that sometimes you do things without knowing the reason why then, but later on you do get your answer. He wasn't sure if this was one of those situations, but he had to know more about Jasmine.

Yes he thought she was pretty, but what else did she have to offer? Was she some gold digging hoochie mama or did she really have her shit together? These questions would often enter his mind while at other times he would often fantasize about what kind of person she was, how it was to be with her, hold her, and to be inside her. It was those feelings that he didn't quite understand himself, because sex never controlled any aspect of his life and he wasn't the "seek and conquer" type. Rather, just a plain boring guy who had fun in his own kind of way. He had been called a closet freak, but he believed that whatever was agreed upon by two people was just that, fun to be had by all as long as nothing was forced or expected upon anyone.

For some reason this woman Jasmine commanded his attention and she didn't even know it. He had to be very careful when being around her for the wrong look could ruin everything he worked so hard to achieve, it wasn't about reality but the perception. It has been said that someone's perception is reality, but the truth is that line only works when it is against you and never for you. Why couldn't people just mind their own business rather than starting some shit over basically nothing?

The last thing he needed was a sexual harassment lawsuit against him or some other unwanted attention, as the corporation would drop him quicker than a bad habit rather than be embroiled in or saddled with a scandal. As he sat sat across from her at the table and slyly looked at those beautiful brown eyes of hers, he begin to feel that they would cause him to wither like a flower in the desert, her mannerism displayed that of a truly first class woman who demanded respect from all she encountered.

In his mind he wanted to be able tell her exactly how he felt, take her in his arms, and passionately kiss her until they both needed to stop for air. There were dreams of how he would lie next to her in bed and explore all the regions of her body as they shared a quiet conversation. Again, it was only a dream and nowhere close to being reality. Besides, she was already involved with someone and even if she wasn't he was not going to break his rule of workplace dating.

Le'Roi started to feel emotions that he had never felt before and frankly he didn't understand it. He had always been the one in control of his emotions and having just met her he didn't understand the effect she was having on him. The way he felt about her was something beyond description, he would give her the world on a silver platter if he could, just for the chance to be with her.

Le'Roi was so confused within himself, one side of his mind kept things in perspective while the other side wanted him to pursue her, what the hell was going on with him as he never experienced anything like this before. It seemed that his mind was on its own track and he couldn't control it when it came to thoughts of her, he definitely didn't need that during the meeting.

Thoughts began to arise as to whether or not she was happy in her current relationship? He knew this was wrong to think that and would never infringe upon another man's territory, but it was simply the way he felt about her and somehow he became determined to find out more about her. Because he had been hurt so much in his past, there was somewhat of distrust with any woman he would meet, usually at the so called hook-up parties where someone would be trying to set him up with someone else, they never went past that evening in most cases. However, he believed that she could change his perspective on all of that; at least that was what he was thinking if there was a possibility of them being together. There was still hope that the passionate and romantic man inside of him could be released without the fear of being taken for granted.

In his fantasy world he envisioned that one day she would come to him and say, "Whatever is it you want, I'm sure I can help you find it". There were no preconceived notions about where things would go, if they ever happened at all. A mere opportunity to show her that he was more than capable of bringing her real happiness was the only opportunity that he would need. Of course that was his fantasy and not hers, so the reality of the situation was that it would remain just that, another unfulfilled fantasy.

Le'Roi found out that Jasmine's significant other's name was Phillip; he started as a low level employee for the company and worked his way up the corporate ladder. It was rumored that Phillip would stab his own mother in the back just to get what he wanted, he was a district manager and had his sights set on being the CEO, and most believed that he would sell his own soul to the devil just to get there. He was a feared man and kept few people near him, you didn't get to know Phillip unless he wanted to know you. Usually when that time came he already knew what he wanted to know about you, his purpose was basically what is it that you could do for him.

Phillip had been married previously and the marriage produced two children. Phillip spent a lot of hours working and trying to climb the ladder, which infuriated his wife. Eventually she left him and took custody of the children. Word on the street is that divorce changed Phillip's personality to the point that most feared him because of his tirades, and propensity to treat people like shit who didn't agree with his policies and philosophies. It was around that time that he started his so-called inner circle, which meant that you were trusted but also expected to kiss his ass whenever he told you to, those were the conditions. The flip side is that he took very good care of his inner circle, of course there were still people who tried to get into it and true to form they usually didn't make it.

Le'Roi didn't really know Phillip nor did he have a reason to get to know him, and as far as a friendship with him that was not desired or even imagined. Le'Roi was in the marketing department; Phillip headed sales, while Jasmine worked in the finance office. So there really was no need for him to meet or know Phillip, as his boss always dealt with the sales department.

Le'Roi often found himself with difficulty staying asleep at night, he didn't know why Jasmine was always on his mind, and hell he would rather have the other thoughts that woke him up dealing with the crap of his childhood. He felt like he was losing control and needed a way out to get his stuff together before he went down a road that was headed for a dead end, and that was not where he wanted to end up. He decided to take a few days off just to clear his head, being as good as he was, no one minded his absence because he would often come back with new marketing strategies whenever he was away. That was his thinking time as he put it, most people didn't understand it, but sometimes you have to walk away from something to better understand it.

Whenever he saw Jasmine with "him", he would become a little jealous and wonder why it couldn't be his arm she was be holding onto. Keeping his composure was the first priority as he knew things could easily get out of hand if he acted on impulses rather than intellectual thinking. The attention was not what he wanted, at least not that type. When the news broke later that they were finally getting married, his heart sank to the lowest depths of the ocean. It would have been better had someone driven a stake into the one thing he had to give her, at least it would have spared him the pain of watching the two of them together. At least he got his answer and although his desire for her still burned inside of him, he pretended to be happy for her, but deep inside he wanted to be with her.

He still didn't understand the hold that she had on him, he couldn't figure out why and she probably didn't even have a clue. He went to a bar later that night just to try and take his mind off things before he took his "thinking time". While there he did get some attention but being as selective as he was, he respectfully declined any invitation of someone wanting to share his bed. The truth being told, he had told more people no than he had said yes to. The question was, would he say no to Jasmine if the opportunity presented itself?

Chapter 8

Word went out throughout the company about the upcoming wedding of Phillip and Jasmine, and as expected, it was an invitation only event which Phillip made damn sure that certain people were invited, while others were not to attend. While he was expected or more so perhaps hoping to be invited to the wedding, Le'Roi was a bit down trodden when the realization hit home that he was not one of the lucky ones to be on the invited guest list. He hadn't done anything to Phillip to warrant being excluded from the special invitation list, but maybe Phillip sensed that perhaps Le'Roi couldn't be trusted, or the real reason was that he found out or sensed the Le'Roi was attracted to Jasmine.

The days all seemed to be the same; Jasmine had Le'Roi captivated, so much to the point that he would sometimes make it his business to go out of his way just to get a glimpse of her in her office. He still didn't comprehend what it was about her that made him so stupefied, and at this point he actually didn't even care what the reason was, he just had to make sure that he was private and discreet in his dealings with her, sort of a private fantasy like situation. It had been six weeks since the hastily called meeting, but she was still on his mind today as if it was yesterday. While he thought he was being discreet, one day she caught wind of what he was doing, but decided to play along and never said anything to him or anyone about it. One day he was passing by her office when she purposely went to the door and stopped him dead in his tracks.

How are you she asked?

Fine, just passing through he replied.

Seems like a long way from your office to just pass through.

Sometimes I do this just to get some exercise in, it helps me with my thinking process and enables me to put pieces together, he said. That sounded so dorky to him that he wished he could have said it another way.

The look on her face said she didn't believe him but was willing to accept his answer, for the moment. Okay, well maybe I will see you later; perhaps he said and walked away. She just didn't know just how much he wanted to see her sooner under the right circumstances, rather than later; he wanted to turn around as he walked away but didn't want to draw any attention to himself. Little did he know that she was standing there watching him walk away, before finally going back into her office and returning to her desk.

Jasmine thought Le'Roi was cute and he did have a lot going for himself, but she could never see herself with anyone other than Phillip, in spite of his ways she didn't want to jeopardize all of the things they had going together, even though she longed for the passion of a real true love relationship. Shortly before they were married, Jasmine's mother needed a major operation and the money just wasn't there. Phillip didn't even think twice about it and made sure that everything was taken care of, for that Jasmine felt like she was totally indebted to him. Having grown up poor, she loved the lifestyle that they lived, even if it wasn't the dream marriage that she had hoped and aspired for.

Phillip liked control and sometimes she felt that he didn't know when to let go of it, having control at work is one thing but the home life is something that is totally different. One day she questioned him about why he felt the need to be controlling at home and he slapped her so hard across the face that she saw stars; she never liked the fact that he hit her, but was willing to accept the fact that he did because she did not want to risk losing everything her lifestyle encompassed, so in respect she tolerated him along with his actions and essentially blamed herself for what happened. In their life it wasn't about her, it was all about him, she didn't like it but she was willing to accept it so as to not go back to the way she grew up.

Her mother adored Phillip and would often tell Jasmine just how blessed she was to find a man as good as him to take care of her. It was Phillip who made sure Jasmine got the job in the finance department, helped with her mother's surgery bills and even paid for a nurse for the follow-up care at her mother's home. Even the house that her mother lived in was owned by Phillip, which he silently used as leverage against Jasmine. For he knew that as long as he held that trump card she was his to do whatever, and if she decided to walk, then her mother would too, out of his damn house! While her mother saw a man in shining armor, Jasmine knew that at times Phillip's anger would become uncontrolled and the mental and physical abuse would soon follow.

It was bad enough that she wasn't able to have children of her own due to a car accident as a child, as that inability made her feel incomplete as a woman at times. Phillip would remind her of the fact that she wasn't able to bear children, which most often occurred during one of their heated arguments. He would say things that hurt her deeply and at times she would rather he hit her than say things, at least the physical pain would eventually go away but the words seem to always stick around. The worse part was when he would get angry because she questioned where he was going and when he would return, she learned the hard way that there were some things that she didn't ask him.

While she may have entertained thoughts of leaving him, she knew that she wasn't going anyplace. Phillip didn't need to remind her of the fact that if she did leave then the job would go and her mother would move out of the house that she was currently in, a mere look on his face said all that needed to be said. So if her mother was comfortable and her lifestyle was fine, she could tolerate Phillip and his so-called ways. That was the kind of influence he had over her and while it may or may not be true, it was what she believed and that was good enough for her.

Still, she longed for the passion of a loving relationship and for some reason that was what she saw in Le'Roi. She had been watching him and knew more about him than he knew of her, he gave her the impression of a peaceful and loving kind of man who adored his woman, but the thoughts of actually being with him were nowhere in her mind. Her mind reflected to the time when Phillip had her consumed with intense passion, the way he would look at her with his piercing eyes, and the gentleness of the way he touched her skin made her want him even more.

She was not sure when things begin to change, but the intimacy slowly started going away until it became what it is today, nothing more than sex. Sometimes she would have rather masturbated than be with him because at least she would continue until she reached an orgasm, whereas he would simply roll over and go to sleep, leaving her unfulfilled.

Thinking back to an unexpected surprise, Phillip showed up at her office after most employees had left work for the day, closing the door behind him, he walks over to her desk where she is sitting. He walks behind her and starts by kissing her on the neck and squeezing her breasts, before his hand reaches under her skirt, moving his hands up her thighs and trying to reach her love box. Initially she tried to fight him off, but the way he touched her with his hands and lips made her want to release the unbridled passion kept up inside of her, besides, she did like the thrill of being dangerously close to being caught. Jasmine opens her legs to allow him better access, and he does his thing as his fingers magically work on her throbbing box before she finally pushes him away. He thinks that she has had enough and is surprised when she took off her panty hose and underwear, it really didn't matter as the panty hose were ruined from the movements of his hands.

Phillip smiles and removes his suit jacket while rolling up a sleeve on his shirt, then continues working his fingers on her wet and juicy pussy, he moved a little more toward the front of the chair as she moves her hips forward to help accommodate his desire to play with her. Phillip loved the fact that her wetness allowed his fingers to slide easily across every part of her pussy. It always amazed him just how wet she would become, and so easily. His middle finger found the gold mine that he was looking for, and he inserted it deep inside her.

She grabs him and kisses him passionately while his middle finger kept going from playing with the clit to hitting her G-spot within the hole that was provided. Faster she whispered, Phillip obliges and watches as she moves a hand under her blouse and squeezes her right nipple. Her body starts to shake from the excitement as she nears climaxing, suddenly she lets out a loud moan as her body jerks forward, sensing this Phillip makes deliberate touches on her sensitive and swollen clit, until her body relaxes and she sits back in the chair.

He makes one last pass on her pussy and moves his finger inside her before taking it out and sucks her love juice off of it. Her eyes are glossed over from the orgasm and he leans forward and kisses her on the lips, she returns his kiss by slipping her tongue in his mouth as she rubs the bulge in his pants. He pulls back and says, "That's for later". He puts his jacket on and makes one last swipe at her juicy pussy with his finger, which he takes and places it in her mouth and kisses her passionately afterwards. He loved to taste the juice of her fruit on her tongue when he kissed her.

Thinking about that moment made Jasmine almost as wet as she was that day Phillip helped to relieve her in the office, but her thoughts in this case were about Le'Roi and she wondered if he would have done something like that. Was he capable of providing the kind of love and attention that she desired? Could he be spontaneous like that and be a risk taker? These questions she asked in her mind, not ever knowing if she would ever get the opportunity to find out. To her it would be a fantasy that perhaps would never be fulfilled, for if she did there was no way that Phillip could ever find out. Time to get back to work she said.

When Le'Roi returned to his office he sat down and thought about Jasmine, of all the people he had come across in his lifetime, what was it about her that made him think of her often. All he knew was that he seemed to be fixated on her and that was not a good thing in his mind, he had to find a way to forget about her and go on with his life. He joined a health club and figured that if he committed himself to a strict regimen of working out, it would help to ease his mind and get her off it.

Chapter 9

Jasmine and Phillip were married and went on a two week honeymoon somewhere in the Caribbean, having status in the company affords you those types of opportunities and he was going to make the most of it. Besides, the company was happy to retain two powerhouse players that contributed so much to its success that they paid for the honeymoon. Of course it was all off the record as the company didn't want to start something it wasn't prepared to continue.

It kind of bothered Le'Roi that he wasn't invited to the wedding, but he knew that it was Phillip's doing and not Jasmine, and more importantly that it was probably for the best. While he really wanted to go he told himself that hell it really didn't matter to him, as he had no involvement with that situation anyway and the closer he became to it the worse things would get; at least that is what he told himself. He was still in denial about his feelings for Jasmine but he just didn't understand why they were so strong for her.

Life deals you a funny hand sometimes and the human aspect of relationships was so difficult to understand. Why is it that the person you are attracted to don't always seem to be attracted to you? This was one of the many questions in life that he pondered in his mind. The second aspect of his thoughts was "why does it seem whenever you meet the right person, there is always something that prevents you from getting together"? It was always the right person at the wrong time, or the wrong person all of the time.

Each time you make a decision about something you take a certain road that is filled with circumstances and different people along the way. You don't know what the situations are that you will encounter or how the people you meet will affect your life, you just know that everyone you meet has a specific purpose, and it is up to you to figure out what that purpose is. Damn this is getting too deep, thinking this hard can give you a brother a brain cramp he thought.

Although he tried to put that aspect behind him, the childhood memories would again surface while he was sleeping, he just couldn't put it all together. He was tired of waking up with things on his mind that he could no longer change, he didn't know why they were so prevalent at this moment. He really wanted to talk to someone about it but his distrust of the mental health community, added with that the stigma associated with seeing a shrink was not something he wanted brought up at the company, as he thought it could hurt his chances for continued success.

Le'Roi's mind was going almost 100 miles per hour it seemed to him, so he figured that he needed a break to get himself together, he checked his calendar and it was clear, so he decided that since he had a couple of weeks before he went on the next trip to pitch his proposal to a prospective client he would take a break to kind of mull things over. The trips were okay and usually involved about five people, one from marketing, sales, finance, planning, and of course a legal representative, just to protect the company's interest. With this in mind he decided to look up an old friend, Sabrina didn't know this but she taught him that use of the Internet was for more than just sexual gratification. Le'Roi found Jerry and it seemed like the two men had never parted, so he booked a flight and went to see him.

Le'Roi spent the next three days doing absolutely nothing; he decided that visiting his old friend Jerry in Dallas was one that not only would rekindle an old friendship, but also gave him a chance to get away from his problems for a while. Jerry was a successful person in his own right, he was a web designer with a few major corporations under his belt, he was also one who loved to party and women were always around him. Le'Roi didn't mind that and just because it wasn't his lifestyle he didn't hang too much with Jerry, of course his friend never took offense to it. Jerry would always tell him, "man you are never going to get your dick wet sitting in the house all the time, well maybe in the shower if you turn the water on", and would laugh as he closed the door on his way out.

Feeling bored and unable to keep Jasmine completely off his mind, Le'Roi went for a walk just to get some fresh air. Thoughts would often fill his head about Jasmine, what she was doing, rather, what he was doing to her intimately? Did she enjoy it? Of course she did, otherwise she wouldn't have married him you dumb ass he told himself. Man this is some crazy shit, I don't even know this woman and here it is I am letting her run my life, what the fuck is wrong with you he asked himself.

The air was somewhat still that night, not really a breeze but not too muggy either. Jerry didn't live too far from the business district so walking was much easier than driving, and far less hassle. Le'Roi saw a coffee shop and figured he would stop for a drink, the place was crowded but there was one table unoccupied, it was only a two-seater but he was alone so it really didn't matter.

He ordered a plain coffee along with a banana nut muffin and grabbed one of the complimentary papers off the counter. He was content with his items when a voice asked "do you mind if I join you, that is if you are alone". Le'Roi looked up and saw a young lady peering into his eyes, no, not at all he replied. Thanks, this is the last seat here and I just have to have my mocha with hazelnut. They introduced themselves and he found out that her name was Debra.

They talked for almost the next hour about anything and everything, things were going really well when Debra said something that took him by surprise, and it was when she asked him "what's bothering you?" Surprised that she would ask that question or even know something was on his mind shocked him, but he didn't respond.

I don't mean any disrespect, but you really look like something is bothering you.

Because he felt comfortable with her, he told her about Jasmine and what he felt for her, all without ever mentioning her name. Well maybe you should remove yourself from the situation if you feel that it could be detrimental to you. That made him feel good, the fact that she could speak to him on a level above the street talk. Le'Roi explained that he didn't want to start over and he didn't see any opportunities available that were comparable to what he had right now. Sometimes, it is in your best interest and not necessarily what you want to do, she said. Man he thought, this woman is really deep with her reasoning.

Well anyway, I must be heading home. Have to get an early start tomorrow, I usually stop here prior to going home to help me relax and unwind from work. Thanks for the conversation and maybe consider what I said. Anyway, I wish you the best regardless, bye. He waved goodbye and watched her as she walked out the door of the coffee shop. He went after her and asked if she was coming back tomorrow? Maybe, we'll see was her reply before she walked away. Debra didn't know it, but she had provided Le'Roi with more of an answer than he had imagined or realized, as her words would weigh on his mind and consume his thoughts.

Le'Roi spent the next day pondering Jasmine and what Debra said to him in the coffee shop, he went to the same coffee shop the next night hoping to see Debra again, but she didn't show up. He sat down and ordered the same thing as he did the night before, his mind was still thinking about the situation of his feelings for Jasmine and what Debra said to him, he knew he had to make a decision one way or another, either get a grip on his feelings or move to another company or position. Finally he made his decision, one that he was hoping that he would never regret. He never saw Debra again but he wanted to thank her for helping him see things on another level.

He felt that his passion for Jasmine had started to become overwhelming and things would came to a head; he knew that in order to save his sanity that he must relocate to another corporate office away from her. He would leave and go to a competitor if he had to but he didn't want to cause anyone problems or jeopardize what he worked so hard to achieve, and he knew both would happen if he stayed in his current position.

When he arrived at work everyone seemed abuzz about something, upon further questioning he found out that a job in the marketing department in Columbia South Carolina had opened up, and he was going to throw his name in the hat for it. This was a perfect opportunity for him, a new location but the same position within the same company, he felt confident that he could get that position and decided to use his calls for favors as leverage.

Using his stature and influence within the organization as well as bargaining, Le'Roi was able to get the job in Columbia, the job had a two-fold purpose, first it would help to reestablish him in another location and present new challenges, but more importantly, he was hoping that it would thereby help to resolve the crisis that dwelled within him. Besides, he felt he had achieved all he could at the current location and felt he needed another area or challenge to conquer just to keep his mind sharp. Yes, a start fresh in a different city and show people that you are not a fluke riding someone's coat tail and also to reaffirm that you are the man, he said to himself.

The day before he departed the organization, he made his rounds to say goodbye. Some people were more than eager to see him leave as that meant the position of "top dog" was open for the taking. During his rounds he passed by Jasmine and stopped her in the hall, he truly had to fight the urge to tell her exactly what he felt inside for her, then again, what would it accomplish? He wanted to let her know that his world was her world and they could be happy together, share the moment of peace and happiness. But it was her peace and happiness that most concerned him most and rather than ruin her good moment in life he just made it a simple take care, and the "I hope to see you again one day" statement.

Nothing special or cute that may draw attention, just a simple statement between two co-workers passing by in the hall. He never saw Phillip and to him that was all well and good, the least he saw of him the better for the both of them. Little did he know or even suspect, that those simple words he said to Jasmine would one day come true. As she turned to walk away from him, he smelled the fragrance of her scent that would stay on his mind for a while, but would later be encountered again. If only he knew just what the future held for him, and her!

Chapter 10

Le'Roi moved to Columbia and settled in rather quickly, while it was considered a small city by northern standards, he found that Columbia still had a lot to offer to someone willing to be adventurous. The city was alive with plenty of places to eat and a lot of places to hang out and party, the best thing was if you were bored or wanted something different, you could always go to either Charlotte or Augusta, as neither was that far away. One could easily learn to like the city of Columbia. Of course one good thing about the city was that it seemed like the women outnumbered the men at least three to one.

While all of that was fine, his most important objective was to reestablish himself in the workplace and get his mind back to business, he had lost a part of himself and didn't understand how he could have let that happen. During the first few weeks he did think about Jasmine and occasionally wondered why he wasn't more forceful in talking with her, too late for that now he thought. On the real he was glad that he was away from her as he could now clearly focus on handling his business.

He still didn't know what it was she saw in Phillip, and it was beyond him to even comprehend the truth. Mostly what was bothering Le'Roi was the fact that during his life he has done his dirt and the one thing he never did was to become involved with or mess with another man's woman. But he reasoned that women are not property and shouldn't be treated as such, why is it okay for a man to fuck whomever he wants and then expect his lady to stay at home and wait for the meager fucking crumbs that he gives her? Then if she did step out on him he only saw what she did while completely ignoring the dirt he was still doing, and then make it seem like she was the worst fucking whore on earth. That stupid alpha male shit that brothers have in their head, all the crap about spreading seed while she keeps her legs closed was complete bullshit, but it was the way most men thought and they did it because the women let them do it.

That was the thinking of Phillip, as he basically felt that women were there for his pleasure and nothing more. While Le'Roi was very respectful of Jasmine, he couldn't stand to see her with Phillip. It was an unwritten rule that whatever happens between the boys stays between the boys, and Phillip had definitely had his share of doing dirt when she wasn't around. There was a time when Phillip held a private function at a strip club and invited some of the guys after work, he loved to host functions and show off his power and wealth.

Everyone was enjoying the show and having fun when Phillip hooked up with a pretty young stripper who was fascinated by his status and wealth. They ended up having a continued encounter as Phillip did the choosing on if and when he saw her, every party he hosted it was made perfectly clear that there was someone there exclusively for him and no one else, even as word spread around the office, amongst the guys of course, no one ever made mention of it to anyone outside of the circle. It was funny how Jasmine never found out about that night and although he didn't like it, he was not about to be the one to spill the beans.

He wondered what the consequences would be for him if he did speak out against Phillip, hell that would not only be stupid but career ending as well. Then again, why would he do that as he was not totally innocent himself, not only did he want to get with another man's woman, but he would also put him down in the process, while it wasn't true that is the way it would have seemed. Back at the office things seemed like they were usual as usual could be, Phillip had shown no indifference to him and the talk around the office was that the only thing Jasmine did for Phillip was have his clothes cleaned and ready for him to go to work in. This talk still fueled the fire in Le'Roi as he didn't like this shit and didn't want to be a part of the office rumor mill.

Phillip invited him to a get-together with just the guys present, he wanted to surprise them but it had to be maintained with the utmost secrecy. Le'Roi didn't understand why he was invited at the time, but eventually it would be revealed to him. The gathering was held at an upscale hotel in the presidential suite, the food was catered and the liquor flowed freely. There were about fifteen guys there and Le'Roi figured they were Phillips most trusted kiss asses, but why was he invited and what was the occasion, Le'Roi thought to himself. The best that he could figure was if he did partake of Phillip's offerings then he would feel that he had something to hold over him and how would he exploit that for his own benefit. Phillip always did things for his own self serving purpose.

There is an old saying that you keep your friends close, and your enemies closer. Maybe that was why Phillip invited him? Not wanting to seem nervous or concerned about his own thoughts, Le'Roi just played along as if he was having a good time. Later as the evening progressed it turns out that Phillip was being considered for the position as Executive Vice President, and if selected he would assume the position sometime in the future, he flaunted that and wanted to show everyone just how good he had it, basically it was a jump on board gathering or be fed to the sharks. Phillip demanded loyalty from those around him and no one ever dared cross him, but Le'Roi didn't give a shit about Phillip or his position.

Approximately two hours after the festivities began; everyone has eaten and slurped down a few drinks when Phillip announces the surprise. The guys started yelling and cheering when Phillip opens the door and in walks twelve women, all are looking good and believed to be from an upscale escort service. Hell Le'Roi didn't do badly by his own standards but damn, these women were hot!

They immediately begin to strip down to their barest essentials when Phillip announces that the "floor is open". That means fellows choose your pickings and the slow guys get whatever is left. Of course there was one that was specifically chosen for Phillip that no one could touch, the rest could share amongst the leftovers. Typical Phillip, that arrogant son-of-a-bitch!

Le'Roi watched as the party with the women began in earnest, but he really had no desire to partake in it at all. He thought about some of the women and wondered what their education level was and how did they get started in the business, but his mind wandered to Jasmine and thought "what would she do if she knew this was happening"? Finally having seen enough, he quietly left. That shit that he just saw didn't even turn him on in the least bit. The drive home was long and desolate, he didn't even complain about the poor driving habits of others as he usually does. This night was different and frankly, he just didn't care.

There were times that he wanted to tell Jasmine everything, but feared that if he did she wouldn't take it in the manner in which he intended, the thing that really bothered him was the talk going on behind her back. His telling her was for informative purposes, but she most likely would take it as him trying to get into her drawers, while that was the truth it was not his motivation for telling her. He couldn't understand how Phillip could just go off for a few days at a time while she sat at home waiting for him to return, what the hell was wrong with the both of them he asked himself? What the fuck, man? He is using her while continuing to have his fun and she is sitting back letting him do this shit to her. What was it that caused her to turn a blind eye to his exploits? Hell if she was my woman she would go everywhere with me, even on business trips. The bottom line to all of this is still the same; it's not his place or business to tell her and frankly, why the hell does he care if she lets him do all this to her?

The next day at the office seemed pretty normal, he saw some of the guys at the party last night and they just smiled at him. He didn't even want to know how it went because the only thing those entire kiss asses were doing was to feed Phillip's ego. His thought was interrupted by a hand on his shoulder; he turned around and was surprised to see Phillip standing behind him.

What happened last night man Phillip asked, next thing I knew you bolted for the door without even partaking of the candy as he laughed. I was just feeling a bit under the weather and didn't want to ruin it for everyone else Le'Roi lied. Well maybe next time you can get a bit more involved as he looked Le'Roi straight in the eye, and said "we keep things to ourselves". We must learn to get along, in order to get along! Le'Roi knew exactly what he meant and simply said, yes, I know. Phillip had invited Le'Roi just so that he could have some dirt on him, but this goody-two-shoe mother-fucker didn't bite. He had to continue trying as he needed someone to replace a member of his inner circle and Le'Roi was it.

What are you two chatting about came a voice, it was Jasmine as she was walking down the hall. Nothing much honey, just talking about sports as usual replied Phillip as he kissed her on the cheek. Le'Roi tried not to show his displeasure but was sure it was written all over his face, hell he never was good at lying so he didn't say anything. I'll talk with you later man Phillip said as he and Jasmine departed. That was the most words Phillip had even spoken to Le'Roi and even though he had invited him to a couple of functions, it meant by no means they were friends.

Le'Roi knew that he had to clear his mind and stop thinking about crap that he had no business or involvement with, to help remedy that he threw himself into his work and besides, most of his thoughts dealt with past issues that couldn't be changed anyway. While most had heard of him through reputation, he still felt that he was being watched to see if he actually lived up to the hype. There were some long days and he didn't mind because the more he was busy the least likely for his mind to wander.

No matter how busy he was, there were the nights where the childhood memories would surface and wake him up. Sometimes it was the same things but usually it was some forgotten things or person. This time it was about the first time he had sex, her name was Renee and she was more experienced than he was. He told her that he wasn't a virgin when he was because he seemed embarrassed to admit it. Most guys on the block had plenty of women and some babies, guess that is where the baby daddy saying started.

Le'Roi knew what he wanted to do with Renee he just didn't know how to go about doing it. His inexperience was evident when she told him to get the fuck off her, and laughed at his clumsiness. She even went out and spread the word about how he didn't know how to fuck; of course the obvious thing to do was to talk shit about how she couldn't take the pain from his big dick. Pretty soon things would die down and your boys will always be your boys, but that taught him a valuable lesson about hooking up with ghetto tramps.

Back to the present, a business trip was coming up in Saint Louis where he and others went to do a sales pitch and financial agreement for a prospective client. He had been at the new location for about eight months and knew that it was his job to make the sale, but didn't know what capacity others were fulfilling as each office had its own agenda, Tom was supposed to go but strangely he didn't join the trip and sent Teresa instead.

It was during a conversation during the trip that he discovered she was new to the financial office. At the conclusion of a marketing pitch one day they met some of the clients in the bar at the hotel they were staying at for a few drinks and some small socialization, the deal was almost assured and everyone was in the mood to celebrate. He had straight bourbon on the rocks while Teresa drank some fancy stuff that he couldn't remember or pronounce, or really cared to know for that matter.

The evening was fine as they both were feeling mellow and he was a little frisky wondering what chance he had to be with her that night. When he walked her to her room the door was slightly ajar so he went in ahead of her to check it out, he turned on the lights and made sure the room was okay. When Teresa came in he closed the door behind her, she placed her items on the table and when she turned around he was right there behind her, and placed his arms around her waist.

She pushed her body up against him which caused his manhood to rise, her hips moved back and forth across his groin before she pulled away and entered the bedroom. He followed in behind her when she turned around and kissed him full on the lips, he returns her passion with a fever.

He starts taking off his coat jacket and she begins unzipping her skirt, Le'Roi looks around and sees a picture next to the bed of a man and a child. Is that your family he asks, yes my husband and daughter. I didn't know you were married, you don't wear a ring? No, besides what difference would it make she responded. At that point Le'Roi says I'm sorry, I can't do this. He composes himself and picks up his jacket then walks out of the room. Teresa is stunned and shocked, but doesn't say a word. Le'Roi didn't like the fact that she was so callous in her response, as if she did this often.

The next morning she didn't show for the usual breakfast gathering, so he ate with the others and went to the final meeting shortly thereafter. They were just about to start when she walked in, he watched her as she went from the door to her chair at the table. Her demeanor was all business today and it showed in everything she did. The carefree fun-loving person that started the trip was absent as she was all about business and nothing else. They closed the deal and grabbed their bags from their rooms for the flight back home. Each time he tried to speak to her and explain his actions she dismissed him with a quickness, that made the flight even longer since they sat next to each other, but neither spoke a word.

Le'Roi hardly saw Teresa after that and it may as well have been for the better, he didn't know what even possessed him to try and get with her other than simply being horny. A year and a half after moving to Columbia, Le'Roi kept true to his reputation as a deal maker, he kept to himself and no one knew his business and he loved that.

One night he received a call from the vice president, who wanted to discuss some impending changes or reorganization within the company. The decision was made to streamline operations and to let some people go as a cost cutting move. Four people were coming in from corporate headquarters to oversee the reorganization which was headed by Phillip, and they would be there for approximately eighteen to twenty-four months. Le'Roi was assured that his job was not on the chopping block, and was asked to simply be a voice of reason to see if things made sense. That was the kind of respect he had garnered from being in Columbia, as his opinion was highly valued. There would be a meeting in a week and Le'Roi would be the front man for the Columbia office to look out for its best interest, and he was planning to do that no matter what Phillip threw at him.

Chapter 11

During the next few weeks things were rather tense around the office, people were concerned about their jobs being eliminated, which in turn caused some of them to distrust each other or try to go out of their way to prove their worth to the company. Le'Roi didn't understand why people were upset at others when they lost their job, especially to those that had nothing to do with the decision. The one thing that puzzled him was why did Phillip come to Columbia, he knew Jasmine's position was the financial piece, but why would a district manager be sent to head a team to reorganize a company that was out of his district?

The reorganization team had arrived and settled into their work areas, of course everything went through Phillip and it still perplexed Le'Roi as to why Phillip would be on that trip rather than back in Atlanta? Maybe he wanted to keep his eye on Jasmine since he knew Le'Roi was there, but there was no way Phillip could know what he thought about Jasmine or felt for her. Yes the feelings had resurfaced but they were no where near the level of intensity that caused him to change jobs. Not my issue he reasoned, if he is so insecure that he can't trust her and that is definitely his problem and not mine to be concerned with.

Often times Le'Roi would walk by and see Jasmine working late in the office with some of the other department personnel, he didn't know what Phillip was doing nor did he particularly care. One day he stood outside the closed door to Jasmine's office and watched her through the window as she worked alone, her hair was professionally kept and she looked stunning. When she got up from the desk he saw she was wearing a skirt with a jacket to match, her legs were very shapely and when she removed her jacket he saw that her nipples were hard as they pressed against the bra and blouse that housed them.

He really became excited when she placed her hands on her breasts and squeezed them before rubbing her swollen nipples. His mind was thinking about how good it would be for him to watch another woman suck on her nipples, would she like it? He was so composed with his thoughts that he unconsciously let his hand move to his groin area and rubs his manhood. She turned toward the door and spotted Le'Roi looking at her through the glass; she quickly dropped her hands and put her jacket back on. Embarrassed now that he was caught, he felt it best to try and play it off as much as possible, he knocks on the door and enters when she told him to come in.

What can I do for you she asked?

Nothing, I saw you working late and wanted to know if you needed anything before I headed out for the evening.

I'm fine and will be heading out shortly myself. I do have a question for you though, I found this file on the Zylander Company but that is all I have on it. The financial transactions are missing and there is nothing in the archives.

I've never heard of them, how long have they been a client?

The file shows records going back for about three years, but I am not sure what it is we do for them or they do for us.

Maybe someone didn't pay attention and just misplaced the file.

Could be, but a large amount of money was paid to them and there's no record trail to show the who, and why. I don't even see a record of approval for the transaction.

I'll look into it Monday; shall I wait for you and walk you to your car?

No you go ahead, I'll be fine.

Le'Roi turns and walks out the door, relieved that no mention was made of the fact that he was standing there watching her. Looking at the way she squeezed her breasts made him curious about her body, he wanted to know if she touched herself, how often, and exactly what she did when she did it. Just another fantasy that will never be fulfilled he thought.

After Le'Roi left, Jasmine wondered how long he had been standing there and just exactly what it was he saw. Her nipples were still swollen and aching to be touched, Le'Roi was a good looking man and it wouldn't have bothered her if he had placed his mouth on them. She missed having the attention and affection of a man, the way Phillip was when they first got together. Being married didn't make much difference, as the passion and excitement was still lacking in their relationship. The marriage was more so for show than love but that didn't matter, she wasn't giving up her lifestyle for anything.

During the next week Le'Roi was still doing counter proposals to retain as many people as he could, what perplexed him was how Phillip would recommend eliminating one position, then come back and create a similar position. What was really astounding was he even had someone already lined up for the job.

One day he and Phillip passed each other in the hall when Phillip stopped him and said, hey man, let's go to lunch, I have some things I want to discuss with you. Not wanting to be around Phillip but also understanding this was his chance to figure out what the mindset of Phillip as far as the reorganization plan went, so he agreed.

Come on, I'll drive Phillip said. Any preference as to what you want?

No, anyplace is fine.

Cool, I know a pretty good Thai place that serves some very spicy food, you can handle that right?

Sometimes, the spicier the better Le'Roi responded.

With a smirk on his face Phillip said "too much can also get you in trouble, if you know what I mean", as laughter pours from his mouth.

They arrive at the restaurant and each orders his meal, Le'Roi didn't want any small talk as he wanted to get right down to business, he didn't trust Phillip before and saw no reason to change his thinking. The place was pretty empty so the services was quick and prompt, as Le'Roi didn't want to be there any longer than he had to.

Phillip breaks the silence and says, hey man, I want you to cut back on all of the counter proposals that you are presenting, it makes things harder than they should be and gives the impression that we aren't working together.

My counter proposals are only in doing what I think is best for the company.

I understand that Phillip said, but eventually you are the one who is going to look bad, you are fighting a losing battle and you must know when to fall on your sword and when to just let things go. Look, I was sent here with specific instructions to accomplish certain tasks and I am going to follow through on them. Remember, I also have a boss who as I must remind you, is higher than yours.

But what I don't understand is why you are eliminating one position only to fill it with someone else.

Basic economics, if you eliminate one position you can bring it back at a lower wage scale, thereby saving money. If you contract it out there are no benefits paid and you make even more money.

While that made sense to Le'Roi, he countered with "but then why not offer that position to the tenured employee rather than someone new"? Yes the pay cut wouldn't be desirable but the opportunity to continue working and supporting one's family wouldn't be entirely interrupted.

Listen to yourself man, you don't give a shit about these people so quit acting like you're fucking Moses parting the Red Sea. It is what it is and if you don't learn to play ball, you may find yourself in a position you won't like.

Meaning?

Damn it bro, if you haven't figured it out yet it is like I told you before, you must learn to get along in order to get along.

The food arrives and all conversation ends, the waitress places the food in front of them and turns to walk away.

See the ass on that bitch, Phillip says. I must see what it is she has to offer.

Wasn't looking Le'Roi responds.

I don't get you man, you just don't seem interested in women. I mean if that's not your thing then that's cool.

Hold the fuck up Le'Roi says sternly.

No man you got me all wrong, I didn't mean it like that, I was just wondering what it is that gets you excited, that's all.

Right now I am purely focused on work and don't have time for a relationship Le'Roi responded.

Shit man I'm married and I still make my time for fun, you should loosen up sometime. Maybe I'll have another party and invite you, that way you can let your hair down so to speak. Besides, every man needs his dick waxed or sucked every now and then; having someone different to do it makes it that much better.

Le'Roi didn't say anything, they finished their meal and Le'Roi headed for the door while Phillip stayed back and talked to the waitress. I'll meet you in the car Phillip shouted to Le'Roi. As he sat in the car he could see Phillip with his hands all on the waitress, before he gave her one of his cards. That was typical Phillip; he didn't do the calling on the initial meeting, the women called him. After that he would call them whenever he wanted to empty his dick, because that's all they were used for in his mind. He could clearly see that Phillip hadn't change at all; he was still the hunter on the prowl.

The ride back to the office was very quiet except for the radio, when they arrived at the office, Phillip put the car in park and looked at Le'Roi and said "remember, what happens between bros is not for hoes". No problem Le'Roi said.

They exited and went into the building, when he reached his office Le'Roi saw he had an email from Jasmine. The message said

"I need to see you as soon as you can get away". Le'Roi called her on the phone but she wanted to see him in person, preferably after work in her office.

Arriving at her office he tapped on the opened door, come in and close the door behind you please. He did as instructed and waited for her to tell him what was going on.

I would like for us to work together on these accounts she said.

That really isn't what I do.

Look, I need someone that is going to give me the straight line when I ask a question and I know that you will do that.

What about the people that . . . she cuts him off before he could finish the sentence.

I really need you to work with me on this, and with the two of us we can get this done pretty quickly. If you are available we can get started next week. I have tried to work with other people but for some reason there seems to be a lot of distrust, so basically you really don't know who to trust and when you ask for something you damn well better be specific.

Let me see what's coming up and I'll let you know, he replied. Of course this will have to be approved by my boss.

Yes I understand that, and thank you Le'Roi, I truly do appreciate this.

Chapter 12

Le'Roi was a bit hesitant to work in such close proximity to Jasmine, not because of what anyone may have thought, but rather because it was due to his own feelings and whether or not they would become as strong as or stronger than they were before. He felt that the time he had been separated from her helped him to regain his composure, but there were also times when he was around her where she still made him melt, he had to keep his feelings in check otherwise things might not turn out so well for him.

Their working together went off with no problems or complications; it was strictly business and nothing more. No matter how many times he smelled the familiar scent of her perfume, it always made him look forward to another time when he could smell it on her even more. While she was strikingly beautiful, she was also a woman who didn't take any mess off anyone. Some figured because she was married to Phillip that she had it easy, but Jasmine was her own woman in every sense of the word, and would let you know it if she felt that you thought otherwise. They exchanged cell phone numbers in the event she needed to discuss some things after hours, Le'Roi didn't like that and preferred to keep work and private life separate, but he was also smart enough to know that he needed an ally and perhaps she could be it.

There were several nights when everyone had departed leaving Le'Roi and Jasmine alone, this was the time that Jasmine usually relaxed herself and was not the strict manner business like, as she would do subtle things like remove her jacket or unbutton her blouse a button or two. Le'Roi liked this part of her as it made her appear more human and approachable, but he dared not insinuate anything other than what it was because the consequences could be devastating to what he wanted, so he had to maintain his professionalism not only because that was what he believed, but also because he didn't want any drama with Phillip.

Did you ever find out anything on the Zylander Company she asked?

No I haven't, the funny thing is that the information on the company seems to be non-existent.

Let me show you what I have she said, she walks to the file cabinet and pulls out a folder, then walks to where Le'Roi is sitting and places the folder in front of him. Leaning over his right shoulder he can feel the warmth of her body close to his, add to that the sweet scent of her perfume causes his mind to begin wandering. He hears her talking but isn't paying any attention to what she is saying, she is now leaning on her arms on the table and as he looks at her he notices that he can look inside her blouse.

The way her breasts filled her bra causes him to become excited, his manhood slowly rising from the thoughts of playing with her supple mounds. His mind is consumed with wondering how they would feel in his hands, how large was the circle that surrounded her nipples. Right now his head is so into her chest that he doesn't realizes that she has stopped talking and is staring at him, he looks rather foolish with his mouth open and he continues to look at the wonderful sight of her breasts in front of him.

That's enough for the day she says as she rises and puts on her jacket,

Huh, I'm sorry what were you saying?

Don't worry about it, she stares coldly at him and then proceeds to quickly exit the room heading to the parking lot after grabbing her things. Le'Roi sits there dumbfounded and then realizes the mistake that he made, he heads out the door to catch her to apologize but he only sees the back of her car. He could kick himself for being so stupid, not stupid for looking at her beautiful chest, but simply by being so careless that he was caught doing it.

Initially Jasmine was upset because she was focused on business and Le'Roi was staring into her blouse, but after she thought about it her temper cooled down and she actually smiled at the fact that another man found her attractive and was not intimated by her. Her mind wondered if he was hard while he was looking at her chest, the questions abounded about the size of his dick and the girth. Was he short and fat or long and skinny? She would love to have a dick that filled her pussy all the way as it rubbed against her side walls. She wasn't paying attention when she almost hit someone from behind, but avoided the accident at the last moment.

The next day when they were working Le'Roi felt very uneasy being around Jasmine but she acted as if nothing happened, still his uneasiness was felt by her and while she could have told him it was okay, she enjoyed seeing him like this. As the days went on it became easier to be around her, and Le'Roi was back to his normal self, but still making sure he was focused on business and not necessarily her body parts.

One night as they were working Phillip stopped by to see how things were going, Le'Roi said okay and that was the extent of his conversation. Jasmine on the other hand brought up the fact that they had no information on the Zylander Company.

Have you checked all the files, Phillip said?

Yes and I can't find any audit trail or approval for any transactions on this client.

Maybe it's just an oversight, have you looked into it Le'Roi?

Yes and I also can't seem to find anything, wondering why suddenly Phillip would treat him like someone important.

Tell you what, let me handle that and I'll see what I can do to resolve this, I'm pretty sure it's much ado about nothing. Phillip wondered who it was that told Jasmine about the missing files, he had to find out.

Phillip walks over to Jasmine and takes the file from her hand, gives her a kiss on the lips and then looks at Le'Roi and says, don't work too late tonight, if I didn't know any better, I'd think that you were keeping her away from me. He follows that with his insidious laugh.

We won't be here much longer, we're going to wrap things up and I'll be out of here soon Jasmine says.

Le'Roi figured that Phillip didn't mind Jasmine working late because that gave him opportunity to go out and do his bidding with whomever, probably the waitress in the restaurant.

Phillip leaves and gets into his car, damn it he yells, and there was no way Jasmine could ever find out the truth about the Zylander Company. He was upset and he knew he had to resolve the issue before it got any further, right now he wanted some relief and he knew exactly whom to call and what he would do to calm himself down. He picks up his phone and when the voice says hello he replies "I'm on my way, not sure how much time I have but be ready". He hangs up the phone and drives off to his destination.

About twenty minutes later he arrives at the place he called, he rings the doorbell and as the door opens he sees that she is wearing a seductive outfit, he smiles and says "how did you know it was me?" I wasn't expecting anyone else and besides, I figured since you are paying the rent for the apartment you have open access. He laughs and says, yeah; well let's keep it that way. She closes the door and he walks in and removes his coat, what will it be today she asks? You know what I like he replies.

She gets down on her knees, undoes his belt buckle and unzips his fly, she pulls his manhood out of his shorts and places it in her mouth and feels him start to grow inside her. She works her mouth all over his tool as if it were a lollipop, licking, sucking, and stroking trying to bring him to climax. Phillip grabs her head and seemingly tries to force his dick down her throat, she pulls back as much as possible but he is excited and damn it determined to make his dick fit down her throat. She gags and starts to push harder to get away from him but he doesn't care, his strokes get faster and deeper until he finally he shoots his load into her mouth. Normally she would have swallowed all of his seed but with the gag reflex going on and the fact that she couldn't breathe, she jerks her mouth away and the semen spills onto his pants.

Bitch, look at what the fuck you did he yells.

I didn't mean to but damn you were choking me and I couldn't breath.

Go clean this shit up; I can't go home like this.

She obediently goes and gets a wet cloth and cleans the cum stain off his pants, when she enters the bathroom to rinse the towel she wonders what has she gotten herself into. This wasn't the same man that was so gentle the last time they were intimate, maybe she needed to get out while she could, but he was paying her rent and she needed that right now. Maybe the next time won't be like this she reasoned with herself.

She goes back into the room and he has his coat on, I have some other stops to make, but I'll see you again soon he says. While she wanted him to stay, she felt it best to just say nothing. He leaves a fifty dollar bill on the table and departs without so much as a kiss for her, her mind is now focused on how he treated her tonight and she basically felt like a cheap ass whore who sold herself for rent money. She goes into her bedroom and lies on the bed, and begins crying until she eventually falls asleep.

Chapter 13

Phillip drives back to the house wondering to what extent and how detailed the information was that Jasmine knew, and if she did know anything whom did she tell, and when did she find out. He was pissed off already because that stupid bitch had him soil his pants; maybe he didn't need her anymore he thought as she had quickly gotten old to him that was the problem with bitches, once you've used them for what you wanted they didn't serve any other purpose. Going back to Jasmine, Phillip saw that everything was going so well with him and his business associates and now she could fuck it all up for him, one thing he knew for sure, he was in way too deep to get out quickly and he may not be let out of the deal even if he wanted to. The flip side of the coin was now he had to contend with Le'Roi and what he may know, man this shit is getting deep he thought. Sometimes when you make a deal with the devil you have to be prepared to pay the consequences.

Deciding that he needed to resolve the issue, he called the other members of his special group in Atlanta for a meeting in Augusta, he felt it was best that they meet on the weekend as questions about being absent from work could cause someone to question what was going on and surely an inquiry would prevail if they met during the week. The least number of people that knew about the situation the better, Phillip was always in control and he wanted to keep it that way.

Augusta was the almost the middle point between the two locations and it seemed like the idea location, as it was far away so as to not arouse suspicion, but close enough that an hour drive or so wouldn't seem like anything unusual.

On his way to the meeting of the people he called earlier in the week, Phillip was already rehearsing what he was going to say and how he would deal with the alleged big mouth once he found out who it was. They met in the parking lot corner of the mall away from the other cars so no one could hear their conversation. Each man was considered an equal partner with no one in charge and everyone had an equal say, all decisions were to be made by a majority of the group, so three out of four solidified all decisions. Any of the four could call a meeting and the words "no exceptions" meant everyone had to be there.

As the four of them assembled Phillip took control as he always did and said "somebody's been fucking talking and I want to know who it is". The guys looked at each other dumbfounded and one named Tom asked "what the hell are you talking about, man?" I just want to know if anyone has been talking to anybody about what we are doing, even if it was a slip-up, I need to know in case we have to cover our tracks. They all looked at each other and said "no".

Somebody's fucking lying and if I ever find out whom it is you won't have any fucking balls left Phillip screamed.

Man what the hell are you talking about said James? You need to keep your voice down, the last thing you want to do is to draw attention to us.

Ain't this some shit said Coleman, you called us all here just so you could accuse us of talking, what's really going on?

I'm just fucking pissed because I think my old lady is on to something and I don't know who she has been talking to besides Le'Roi, I just want to make sure we are safe.

Oh, is that what this is about replied James.

What's that supposed to mean Phillip said? James looked around and realized he spoke too much, nothing man, it was nothing.

Oh no motherfucker it meant something and goddamnit you are going to tell me what it meant or I am going to beat the shit out of you Phillip said as he made a move toward James.

Coleman stepped between them and said "I told you we couldn't trust Le'Roi", and now he may be in bed with your wife and we all could get screwed.

First off, Le'Roi is NOT in bed with my wife and the next time you talk to me in that tone of voice I am going to kick your motherfucking ass, Phillip screams.

Hey cool down man, we don't need to draw attention to ourselves said Tom, looking around to see if anyone was watching them. Obviously there is something else going on but that's your issue man. Kicking the shit out of us isn't going to make your problems go away.

I'm just saying that if you are worried about your old lady and what she knows then maybe you should be checking on YOUR old lady and not us Tom said, trying to cool things off before they got out of hand. Phillip was hot right now as he felt that he was losing his power base with the guys. No one had dared talk to him in this manner before. He wanted to lash out when he realized that the statement did make sense, perhaps he did blow this out of proportion and she didn't know anything about his dealings. What does she know Phillip thought to himself, he had to find out but how could he do it without arousing suspicions, a private investigator could uncover too much, he had to figure this out and do it quickly.

The party departed and as usual no one mentioned anything about whatever was said or transpired, as one person speaking could ruin everything that was being worked. When it was all over, he would deal with each of them accordingly, he would get his power base back and they will never speak to him like that again.

The drive for Phillip was unusual; his normal demeanor would be to talk to one of his bitches and when he was coming over to get some ass. His entourage included married and single women, none of which he cared about as long as they kept him happy in the bed and if she refused, he simply moved on. To make sure that his women did what he wanted he kept them compensated, so if he left then the compensation package left as well. He was immersed in his own thoughts about Jasmine and what she knew when his phone rang, it was Jasmine and she wanted to know when he would be coming home, why came his response. Just wanted to know when I should have dinner ready she said. I will get there; when I get there he replied, I have some business to attend to he said and hung up the phone.

That phone call pissed Phillip off to the highest degree and his thoughts shifted from what Jasmine knew of his operation to sex, for some reason whenever he wanted to release some frustration his mind always turned to that and how he wanted it. Right now he was thinking which one of his whores he wanted to fuck; he always seemed to think better with an empty dick. He dialed a number and when the voice on the other end said hello he replied "hey baby, I'm on my way over". Not now she said, I have some errands to run.

Do that shit later; I will be there in thirty.

I really can't see you right now, it will have to be later she said and hung up the phone.

What the fuck is going on Phillip thought, who does this bitch think she is? First the guys get flip at the lip and now this bitch thinks she can do the same. He headed to her house to see what the hell was going on, he had no intention of going to the door, he just wanted to know the real reason for her not wanting to see him, and he was going to find out what was happening even if it meant he had to follow her.

Phillip parked down the street in a position where he could see the door; he opened the glove compartment and took out a small pair of binoculars. He kept them there so whenever he went on his excursions to check up on the guys he could see whom they were talking to, in this case he didn't know why he pulled them out but he did anyway. He also kept a gun for protection, you never know when an occasion would come that you would need it so he wanted to err on the side of caution. He called her again several times and each time she never answered the phone, the stupid bitch didn't realize that he could see she was home.

About twenty-five minutes went by when he saw a car park outside of her door, a man walks up and rings the door bell, when the door opens he sees that she is wearing a sun dress and greets him with a kiss before closing the door behind them. Phillip is now boiling, that's why she couldn't see me, and she has some other motherfucker that she giving the pussy to. Although Phillip was mad, he had to be content to sit there and wait until the guy left, and then he would go in and deal with her. He had to leave an impression on her, one so severe that she would never place him on the back burner again. His mind started thinking of how he wanted to hurt her so much that she would beg him to stop, yes, she needed a lesson.

A little over an hour later, the man leaves and Phillip sees that she is now wearing a bathrobe when she stepped on the porch, she kisses him goodbye and he enters his car and drives off. After his car is no longer in view, Phillip gets out of the car and walks to her house and rings the door bell, the door opens and she says did you forget something? Those words would echo in her head for when she saw Phillip she knew that she had messed up, as fear struck her when he slammed the door shut.

A stinging burn struck on the right side of her face before she felt another one on the left side of her face, as he tried to slap the shit out of her, literally. Phillip grabs her and shakes her violently while yelling that he plays second fiddle to no one before pushing her down on the floor. She tries to crawl away but he grabs her bathrobe and pulls it off her body, he undoes his pants and lets them fall to the floor, exposing his semi-throbbing manhood, watching her squirm and try to crawl away excites him all the more and causes his manhood to become fully erect.

Where the hell did she think she was going? Her ass was his and he was going to let her know just how badly she had made a mistake by putting him off. He is excited and pissed off at the same time, damn it he came for some ass and he was going to get it before he left. Yes, he was going to show this bitch who the fucking boss is. He paid her fucking rent and she has the fucking nerve to put him off and fuck somebody else, that's the problem with bitches he would usually say, you let them get away with something and the next thing you know they are trying to run all over you.

Phillip grabs her leg and pulls her toward him, causing her to get rug burns on her body, he did this because he was determined to teach this bitch a lesson that she would never forget. He enters her from behind while grabbing her neck with his left hand, this wasn't about intimacy at all, hell it wasn't even fucking, and this bitch was going to pay for putting him on hold for someone else. He strokes his dick ruthlessly inside her already swollen pussy that was beat up by the guy that left her place before Phillip ranged the doorbell, she pleads with him to stop thinking that if she had a chance to explain herself then he would understand, but her begging seems to only spur him on.

Under normal circumstances he would have wore a condom, but this was an exception as his mindset was only about causing her pain and not necessarily protection or pleasure for himself. It really didn't matter to him as he was about to teach her a lesson that she would never forget, if she knew what he had in store for her before she fucked the last guy she wouldn't have done it. Phillip leaned back and puts his arm around her waist to pull her to her knees, he pushes himself into her trying to put every inch of his dick into her body.

Each time she tried to pull off him he would just push back harder, eventually her resistance slows and she lets him do what he has to do. She is crying and hurting from him when he gets upset because he is not hurting her the way he wants to. He starts to get even more upset when he looked down and saw her little brown hole that looked so inviting. If she thought she was hurting now he said to himself, she will wish that was all I was doing to her. He reaches around with his hand and rubbed her pussy, it was soaking wet when he touched it and then moved his hand to her asshole. The first time he did it she didn't move, but when he did it the second time she begin to panic.

Sensing what he wanted to do, she again tried to pull of him but his grip was too tight on her, Phillip reached around again and felt her wetness before moving his hand back to her asshole for the third time. Phillip then pushed her down on the floor and spread her legs with his before forcefully pushing his dick in her ass, she screamed and begged him to stop, as she tried rolling from side to side, anything that would get him out of her ass. But he kept going like a possessed man oblivious to anything going on around him, the more she fought against him the more pain it caused and he liked that. She tried to wiggle from underneath him but it was all to no avail, his grip was just too tight. She felt him slow down and thought that it was over, at least that what she hoped but hopes can always be dashed, as she would soon find out.

Phillip grabs her by her shoulders and waist and pulls her up on her legs as he stroked himself roughly in and out of her asshole, while he totally ignores her screams and pleas to stop, little did she know it but this is what gave him pleasure and excitement. He didn't care how much she was hurt, now maybe the bitch will learn her lesson. Finally, he reached his point and pulls his dick out of her ass and pushes her to the floor before he unloads his cum on her back and buttocks. Right now she is sobbing pitifully as he showed no mercy on her body; Phillip reaches for her bathrobe on the floor and wiped himself off with it before throwing the bathrobe down on top of her.

He looked down at her as she lay on the floor sobbing, obviously in pain not only from his rough handling, but also from the point that he had such little regard for her as a person. Stupid bitch he thought, but he didn't care, this was nothing but a piece of ass to him and he was not going to fuck it up by showing emotion. Phillip fixed his pants and straightened his clothes, he turned to walk away but stopped and said "I am nobody's second string player bitch, and if you haven't figured it out by now then now maybe you will need another lesson". Tell that motherfucker your ass belongs to me, he yelled as he walked out of the door and back to his car.

Although she was hurt physically by Phillip's rough sex play, more importantly emotionally she was devastated because no man had ever treated her with such disrespect before. This time was worst than the last time he stopped by and she was feeling as if things were only going to get worse. The only thought in her mind was how would she pay him back for hurting her, she wanted his ass to hurt just as much as he had done to her. Yes, she needed a plan and she wasn't going to stop until she carried it out, getting even with Phillip was her goal.

Now that he had that business out of the way, it was time to focus on the other business at hand with Jasmine. Again Phillip's mind went back to what it was she knew, when she knew it, and how much did she actually know, and whom did she tell? These questions had to be answered and answered very soon, the last thing he wanted was for the other guys to lose confidence in him as that would jeopardize everything that he had worked for and hoped to achieve. While scheming up his plan was easy, Phillip never expected the problems that have surfaced to ever come into play. No matter, he had to deal with them or they would sure come back to haunt him in the future.

That problem was for later, right now he had to figure out what his wife knew, as she could hurt him in ways he had never imagined.

Chapter 14

The reorganization team had been there almost three months, so far eight positions had been slated for elimination and three rewritten for a lower pay scale. While no changes occurred just yet, Phillip was determined to get the new hires in place as soon as possible, that way they can provide some type of continuity prior to the old person departing, sort of a transition type deal.

Jasmine and Le'Roi stopped working together for about two weeks, as his attention was needed in other places. He was the go to kind of guy that the vice president loved having around, and once he was given a task the vice president never followed up or questioned whether or not it was done, for he knew that it would be. While this made him valuable to the company it was also wearing Le'Roi thin, but he never made mention of it and simply made the best of the situation.

Phillip continued to watch the woman's house to see if she had learned her lesson or if she needed another one, during the next couple of weeks he would stop by unexpectedly just to see what she was doing and who was there? Each time he found that she was alone and she treated him with the kind of treatment that he required, he wanted to be catered to on every aspect and she made him feel like he was the only man in her life. He wasn't intimate with her each time he was there, but whenever he was she did whatever it was that he wanted, as she was used for his pleasure and he was not there to provide it for her. Eventually he figured he would get tired of her and toss her away like a piece of trash, he would still pay her rent up until then but soon she had to go and he would find another piece of ass to play with.

It was unusual to work on a Saturday but Jasmine felt it best since they kind of fell behind on their work when Le'Roi was pulled away for other duties. She wished she had at least one or two other people with his caliber of skills to help complete the tasks, the ability to be perceptive and to provide a valid argument as to why something should or shouldn't be done was hard to come by and that was his specialty, at least it appeared that way.

They started that morning working on catching up and soon lunch time came around, they ordered something from a nearby deli for delivery and continued working until the food arrived. They ate the meal almost in complete silence and were near being finished with the meal when Jasmine asked the question:

Why is it that you haven't gotten married Le'Roi?

Just haven't found the right person yet, besides I want to make sure my career is firmly established first.

You don't think that you are established now? Man what is it you are trying to achieve?

Just wanting to make sure that I have done all I could to see how far I can go, that's all. There are no preset conditions or positions that I am striving for.

Sounds to me like you are trying to be the CEO.

No, that's too much work but it does sound nice. (They both laugh).

Do you think I'm attractive she asks?

The question takes Le'Roi by surprise and he didn't know what to say. He didn't want to tell his true thoughts and feelings but on the other hand he did.

I think you're cute and a very good business partner.

So you're not attracted to me at all?

I see you as another professional, that's all.

Funny, I wouldn't have known that from the time I saw you looking through the window, and the other time when you were looking into my blouse.

If Le'Roi could have blushed that would have been the time to see it. He didn't know that she would bring those things up, and thus was speechless.

It's okay; you were just being a man.

To be honest Jasmine, I do find you attractive but I wanted to maintain a professional relationship with you. Besides, you're married now and I have to respect that. He wanted to tell her so many things at that moment, about his true feelings, the things that Phillip was doing, and just how much he wanted to be up inside of her.

Okay, fair enough. I would prefer that we keep this conversation to ourselves she said. And on that note let's get back to work

They each gathered their respective trash when Jasmine walked by him and brushed her chest against his shoulder as she headed to the trash can, he turned to look at her and when she walked back by he reached out and took her in his arms and kissed her firmly on the lips.

She pulled back and yelled "what the hell are you doing"?

But I thought . . . .

You thought what? I simply asked you some questions and you took it to another level. You know what, leave, just leave! I will do this by myself. You really disgust me!

Le'Roi was now upset because he felt she had led him on but to say that he was disgusting when her husband was out there fucking every hole that he could get into made him mad. So I'm disgusting, what about that fucking husband of yours? He tries to get into every pussy that he sees! Le'Roi realized that his anger got the best of him and he said things that he shouldn't have said, but he couldn't take it back.

Jasmine grabbed her belongings and left the building, Le'Roi followed her to the elevator apologizing profusely, but she acted as if she didn't hear him and wasn't in the mood for his apologies.

Le'Roi wondered what she would do, would she file a sexual harassment claim against him. That would be easy for him to deal with compared to her telling Phillip about what happened. Why the hell did I do that Le'Roi asked himself. He was pissed at his own stupidity and now he had to deal with whatever became of it. Le'Roi spent the rest of the weekend pondering what was going to happen, he called Jasmine's cell phone but always received her voice mail. He never left a message as he didn't know if Phillip would listen to the messages, if Phillip did call then he would say it was about the work they were doing.

Jasmine didn't come to work on Monday as she took a personal day, Le'Roi figured he would no longer work with her as the best thing to do was to separate himself from the situation. He would tell her that the next time he saw her.

It had been about four days since the incident and Jasmine still had not come to work, while he wasn't really concerned about her, he wondered what was going on. This was so unlike her to not be engulfed in her work, a bit of panic enters his body as the unknown of what was going to happen filled his thoughts.

Finally Jasmine came back to work and carried on as if nothing had happened; at least she hadn't said anything that he knew of. He walked to her office and asks to come in, she allows him to enter and he immediately went into apology mode. Jasmine accepted his apology and said that he was forgiven and the incident was forgotten about.

Over the course of the next few weeks things really did seem to get back to normal between the two of them, while it seemed okay he was still mindful of the way he approached her. Le'Roi felt that he had dodged a bullet and he wasn't about to make the same mistake again. He had to find a way to temper his emotions for her and the fear of a sexual harassment charge definitely helped, but didn't totally eliminate his thoughts of her.

One day he arrived home after work and saw there was a message on his voice mail; it surprised him even more when he discovered it was Jasmine. She wanted him to call her on her cell phone; he was puzzled as to why she didn't call his cell phone but rather wanted him to call her. Le'Roi was hesitant as he didn't know if he should call and what was it she wanted to discuss with him since he had been with her for the better part of the day; these questions dogged him for almost an hour before he picked up the phone and called her number.

Hello?

Hi Jasmine, it's Le'Roi; you wanted me to call you?

Yes, I would like to meet with you; can you meet me at the Charity Inn off Cherry street tomorrow afternoon?

Charity Inn, isn't that a motel?

Yes it is, but it is important that I meet you to discuss something. Can you make it?

Yes, around what time?

About 2:00 PM, I'll be in room 108

Okay, I'll be there

One last thing Le'Roi, please keep this strictly between us.

No problem, you know how discreet I am he replied.

Okay, I will see you then.

Can you tell me what this is about?

I will tomorrow, goodnight.

Goodnight.

What does she want to talk about at a motel he asked himself? He hardly slept during the course of the night wondering what on earth she wanted to discuss with him. Finally he let it go and went to sleep.

Le'Roi left for an assumed appointment with a potential client and headed to the Charity Inn for his meeting with Jasmine. Not the one to be late, he arrived a bit early and parked the car in a not so assuming location, just as a precaution. He knocked on the door and as it opened he didn't see anyone, come in she said. As he walked in the door he wondered where she was and as he reached to close the door behind him he saw that she was standing behind it.

He saw that she was wearing the most elegant lingerie and before he could say a word she grabbed him and kissed him full on the lips. This startled him as he could not believe what was happening, especially in light of the situation that occurred a few weeks ago. He wanted to pull back away from her but her lips felt good pressed against his, and the warmth of her body sent sensations all throughout his manhood. He puts his arms around her and finally starts to reciprocate the kisses that she has been giving him. The feeling of his tongue sliding against hers was beyond imagination, as she would alternate between kissing him and sucking his tongue, this gave him goose bumps. She removes his suit jacket and pushes him on the bed, he tried to ask a question but she simply pressed her fingers against his lips while undoing his zipper and exposing his dick.

Moving down to his hips, she undoes his belt and loosens his pants to further expose his goodies. Slowly she kisses his lower belly and legs before sliding a tongue around the base of his manhood, causing it to throb and become fully erect. Her mouth gently covers the head of his dick before going deeper into her mouth, as she began moving her head up and down on his long hard shaft.

He raises his head and sees just how beautiful she looks, not because she is sucking his dick, but just how truly beautiful she really is. He never saw her lips as the kind for sucking a dick, but rather for kissing and admiring. Her mouth is everywhere in his groin region, licking the bottom of his nut sack and gentle sucking his balls makes him want to explode from the excitement.

Le'Roi doesn't believe this is truly happening, he was never the type to do this and his desire to have her stop just wasn't there, as his fantasy was about to become a reality. Suddenly she stops what she is doing, this causes him to think that now she is having second thoughts about what is being done and wonders what the hell is going on. She removes her clothes and tosses them to the side.

He watches as she grabs a condom, she tears the package opened and slips it on him, then climbs the bed and straddles him. The warm sensation of her pussy on his dick sends chills up his spine as she rides his tool, slowly at first and then she thrusts herself hard down on it.

He grabs her hips and meets every thrust with the same passion and intensity that she is giving him until her body erupts with a strong orgasm. Her body trembles as she releases the passion that had built up inside of her, watching her causes him to spill his own load, as she collapses on top of him while his dick throbs out the last bit of seed left in the shaft.

Chapter 15

After their breathing has settled down he is trying to come to grips with what just happened and more importantly, how he could have allowed himself to not maintain control. She rises up off him as his now limp dick slides out of her, he heads to the bathroom to clean up as he still had on his suit pants and didn't want them soiled. He removes his clothes before jumping into the shower, when he finished he heads back into the room where he finds her lying in the bed under the covers. He crawls in on the other side and doesn't say a word. The silence is broken when she says "thank you for coming", they look at each other and he replies "which time"? This causes them to break out in laughter.

When the laughter dies down Le'Roi says, okay, what is going on, especially with what just happened here?

I just wanted to have a little fun

So you used me for your fun?

No it's nothing like that at all, let's just say that I did some thinking and wanted to act on my feelings.

Jasmine you know that we can't do this, it could change the dynamics of everything.

I think that we can still be professional at work, and enjoy each other whenever we can.

So you want me as a fuck buddy so to speak.

No I don't want a fuck buddy, I want someone to romance me and show me passion. I see that in you.

But how can I truly show you passion when you belong to someone else?

So you're telling me that you didn't feel anything with what just happened?

Okay I did feel something, but I'm not sure that I can provide you what it is you are looking for. Things might get out of hand, feelings get involved and complications set in.

Your feelings are already involved; I knew it the day you kissed me. I just didn't know mine would come to surface so quickly, I have always thought you were good looking and wondered what it would be like to be with you. You don't go out and sleep with anybody and you're very private, I like that and I also know that whatever happens between us you will be discreet with it.

I'm not sure about this he said, what if Phillip finds out?

That's why we have to be discreet.

Looking at the clock he realized that he had to stop by the office before going home. They made love one more time as he was trying to show her that he also has skills. When they finished he got up and got dressed, kissed her on the lips and walked outside. He instinctively looked around to see if anyone was there, he didn't know whom he was looking for, but wanted to see if anyone saw him. Jasmine showered and left shortly after him, headed to her house.

Later that night Le'Roi received a text message on his cell from Jasmine thanking him for participating in the "meeting" today, and how she was looking forward to the next one. He just smiled and didn't reply back.

Life at the office seemed to return to a bit of normalcy, but Le'Roi was still cautious of Phillip and thus it kept him on his guard. He wasn't sure if things would ever come to a head over his counter proposals but he knew that Phillip was a snake and couldn't be trusted, the statement Phillip made about having to "get along, in order to get along" still stuck in his head and he couldn't figure out what he was talking about.

He was pretty confident that he didn't know about him and Jasmine so what could it have been? He had other things to worry about and needed to focus back on the business aspects, he hadn't signed a new client in almost a month. He had never gone that long without closing a deal, could it be that the relationship between him and Jasmine was weighing on his mind? Or was he afraid of what might happen if Phillip found out he had been with his wife, even if it was only one time.

The ringing of the telephone interrupted his thoughts and brought him back to the present, it was a potential client that wanted some exposure for an interior decorating business. Le'Roi knew he had to break his losing streak so to speak and agreed to meet with the owner for some marketing strategies, and show her how he could gain her more exposure.

Le'Roi and Jasmine continued their conversations; their relationship grew from one of caution to one of an amazing friendship. Le'Roi found it was strange how they could work along side each other during the day, and then just talk for hours after work and never get tired of talking with each other. Yes the conversation level was different as he had never experienced anything like this in his life and according to her; he made her feel alive again. He even went so far and told her how he wanted to have anal sex with her, and while she didn't say anything it did pique her curiosity listening to him describe it in full detail.

She shared that while she and Phillip lived together, they had not been intimate in four months, and he apparently told her that she didn't excite him anymore. But for the sake of their reputations and image they needed to stay together and "act" like they were married. This rule only applied to her as he often went about his rituals of parties and escorts with no thought of her.

Jasmine mentioned the time when Phillip flew in from an overseas conference in Europe, even though he arrived at midnight she had him a nice bubble bath waiting along with some chilled white wine. She wanted him to relax in the bath and she planned to massage him afterwards to remove the tension of the flight. Phillip promptly came in, took a shower, changed clothes, and left the house without so much as a word to her. He came home that afternoon and acted as if nothing had happened, and went straight to bed to get some sleep.

She would often look at herself as being the problem and would try to do things to please him at home, while putting up that strong exterior at work. Jasmine even went into a depression and was taking antidepressant medication to help lift her spirits, when Phillip found out he wasn't supportive in the least bit, he just laughed at her and called her a junkie for taking medication. It might have been a good thing she was on the medication because had she not been he might have gotten a razor to the face.

She wasn't a violent person, she just became tired of being treated like nothing and wanted more out of life. However, she knew that Phillip had all the keys to whatever road she took and he would use that as leverage against her, the house that her mother lived in, the cost of the operation that saved her mother's life, she felt indebted to Phillip and just because things were not what she wanted, she was not going to act like a fool and leave him, at least that is what she believed. When it was all said and done, she still wasn't going to give up her lifestyle and go back to struggling like she was before they met.

And as she thought about all of these things, a smile came across her face. Not because of the way she was treated by Phillip, but how Le'Roi made her feel passion and desire again. Le'Roi didn't demand anything of her and she didn't of him, they were content to just enjoy each other's company with no expectations of anything from each other. She loved the way he looked at her, even when passing each other through the halls. No words had to be spoken to understand just how each one felt about the other, the chemistry they shared was like no other, and she loved every bit of it.

It had been almost a month since their meeting at the Charity Inn, perhaps it was time for another so that she could see if he could really live up to what he was telling her. She called him on his cell to see if he would be up for another "meeting"? Of course he said yes and told her he would take care of the details and let her know the when and where.

Where will he be, Le'Roi asked?

Let me worry about him; don't ruin a good moment by mentioning his name she replied.

Sorry, wasn't trying to upset you, what time is good for you he asked?

You tell me when and where, and I will make sure that I am available.

Cool he responded, I'll be in touch. Later that day she sent him a text message that said "I would love to suck your dick". When he received the message he wasn't in a position to respond, but later he responded with his own text message "and I would love to eat your pussy". He never gave any thought after that and set out to put his plans in motion.

His plans had to be of the utmost attention to detail, for he wanted to make sure that everything was just perfect for her. Because he saw her as the perfect lady, and felt that she should be treated as such. He loved to look at the beauty of her face; her lips seem to just beg him to kiss them, something he felt he could never get tired of doing.

The way the hair on the side of her face came down just drove him crazy with excitement, she hated the hair on her face but he loved to look at the sideburns as he thought they were oh so sexy. The arrangements were made and he gave her the information, Charity Inn room 110. He wanted 108 to recapture the moment they first shared but it was taken. They would meet in a couple of days during the afternoon so as to not arouse suspicion, especially with Phillip.

While he wanted her very much, he felt compelled to mention to her how he felt about the situation and mainly Phillip. Each time they would discuss it she would become very agitated, she didn't understand why he didn't trust her on this; it wasn't that he didn't trust her, his concern was that snake in the grass named Phillip and felt that perhaps she was underestimating his capabilities. Of course in her mind Phillip didn't give a fuck about her so whatever she was doing was her business. Not wanting to push her away, Le'Roi said "okay, I will trust you on this but I am just a bit nervous and think that you need to be careful and not let anything slip up".

Usually when Jasmine was upset by Phillip's actions or his words, she would get down on herself. Although he had done it many times before, it never lessened the pain she felt from the way he treated her. Wanting to feel better, she called the one person that she knew could lift her spirits. Hello? Hi baby, hey darling came his reply. Doing anything special today he asked.

No, he is out doing his thing and I am here doing nothing.

Too bad, maybe you should go and do something for yourself.

Not to put a damper on things, but have you given any thought to what we are doing and how often we do things he asked? What do you mean she said? I mean Phillip is not a slow guy and you may think that he doesn't care about you but he may be checking up on you without you even knowing it. Right now he may be okay since we are working together but at any point he could become suspicious.

Why are you worried about what Phillip may be doing, you should trust me and what I tell you she said loudly.

I do trust you baby, I just think that you underestimate him and I just don't want to be a source of drama in your life or see what you worked so hard for taken away from you.

Then you need to trust me when I tell you that everything is okay she said. While she may had sounded confident, Jasmine knew in the back of her mind that Le'Roi was right, he had proven that on a couple of occasions when he told her that some things were going to happen and although she didn't believe him, they did happen.

Just like the gentleman he was Le'Roi never said the "I told you so" story, he simply asked how can we get past this, as if her problems were his very own. This is what made him so special to her, his uncanny ability to listen and repeat back what was said, but his willingness to show you that you were not alone with whatever you were going through. He was a wonderful man and she desired to be with him whenever she could, as he really made her feel special.

If you tell me to trust you then I will, Le'Roi said. They continued their conversation for the next hour, for whenever they talked, they never needed any particular conversation to have as a topic; they could talk about the weather for an hour and not realize that much time had elapsed. Of course at some point a sexual topic would enter the picture, but because of the admiration and respect they had for each other it was never taken as something negative.

Each person knew the limits of the relationship and both were content to just be there for each other, even if it meant that nothing physical could ever happen between them. So, when do we get together again Jasmine said? I am off on Thursday; can you break away from the job for a few hours? Yes I can she said, but one day I want to go someplace when I can walk down the street with you and act like you are my own without the worry that someone might see us. Okay, one day we will do that Le'Roi said. Of course it won't be around here.

Promise she asked?

Promise he said.

Chapter 16

Jasmine sat at the computer on her desk and was looking through some emails making sure that nothing was overlooked, what she was really interested in were the responses from the emails she had sent to other members of the company inquiring about the Zylander Corporation. At this point, neither she nor Le'Roi had been able to find any information on the company, and it appears almost as if the company didn't exist. If that were the case, then why do we have recent transactions for them she asked herself?

Phillip said he would handle things with the file and she was content to let him do that, but she wanted to help him and didn't see anything wrong with her also working it, as a resolution on this issue would help her so that she could close the case out and work towards finalizing the balancing of the books, and allow her to present the final cost savings estimate of what the company would realize when the reorganization was all said and done.

When Phillip got wind of Jasmine sending emails to other members of the company inquiring about Zylander, he knew he had to intervene and stop her before she found out anything more than what she already knew. Of course he still had no idea what she knew or how far she had gone in or out of the company in an effort to find out. Phillip tapped into her work email to see whom she had contacted, he called all of the people she sent the email to and basically told them that the situation was taken cared of and there was no need to follow up.

He was about to look at her calendar to see what she had planned when a call came though on his cell, it was his "client" and he wanted a meeting very soon. What's this about Phillip asked? Just be here in forty-eight hours. Phillip didn't like being bossed around like that, but he also knew the consequences of his not participating. He called the travel agent and booked his flight, he didn't want anyone involved so he took care of his own arrangements. He was about to close out Jasmine's email when he saw a new entry into her calendar, it was a blocked time for a meeting with Le'Roi.

This was very strange because they were working together so why would they require a meeting time? Phillip's thought was they were going to do some more digging into Zylander, but what are they doing and where are they going? He knew that he had to deal with this when he returned, but he had to make sure that he was prepared to face his client first. His plan was to fly down early that morning and return in the afternoon or later that evening, as he had to find out what the meeting between the two of them was about. What Phillip didn't know was that Jasmine set up the meeting to ensure that there were no interruptions for what she had intended to happen with Le'Roi.

The morning of the meeting, Phillip drove to the airport and pondered what the nature of the meeting was with his client. Phillip's plane landed at the airport and he is greeted by a driver with a car, who is waiting to take him to the designated location, which was never announced in advance. The ride to the location was a quiet one, the driver didn't speak and each time Phillip tried to start a conversation he was ignored. He was hoping to get some kind of clue as to what the urgency of the meeting was about. They arrive and two men meet the car outside a building, both are packing heat, which was normal for any meeting with the client but there was some tension in the air today.

They enter the building and Phillip sees that is was an old factory of some sort, there are other men in the hall and some looking out of windows. Phillip is led to a room and stopped in the center, he sees three men sitting at a table discussing something between them as if he isn't even in the room; there isn't much light but he senses that there are others in the room but figured they were security personnel.

Phillip, glad you could make it one of the men said.

Yes sir, it's not a problem Phillip replied.

But we do have a problem another said, it appears that someone close to you is digging into our business and we don't like that. There has been talk about some cooperation with the federal agencies and frankly it makes us nervous.

Phillip was silent as he wondered how they knew what Jasmine was doing, he knew they had contacts and resources but now he wondered if someone on the inside was feeding information to them. I will take care of it he said, assuming it was Jasmine that was the problem, but who could it be that is cooperating with the fed's was beyond him.

I can't express the importance to you of taking care of this quickly, much is at stake and we don't take kindly to people interfering into our affairs. You assured us that we would have a good business arrangement with no complications and now we have this, one of the men said.

Things are okay, I will resolve it quickly. No one will ever find out Phillip said.

I hope so, because if it does come to that you can expect this, a light shines on the left side of the wall and Phillip sees a man with his hands tied hanging from what looks like a hook from the ceiling. He wasn't wearing a shirt or shoes and his body had been badly beaten, his face was a bloody pulp, Phillip isn't sure if the man is dead or alive or what he had done to deserve that treatment. His hands were wrapped in bandages and Phillip assumed that maybe one or two of his fingers were missing. One thing he knew for sure is that he didn't want to end up like that poor piece of shit. Suddenly a man steps out from the shadow and cuts the man across his chest with a long knife that almost looked like a machete, the man's screams confirmed that he was still alive, but for how long. Phillip looks back at the table where the three men are sitting.

This is how we deal with problems and as you can see, we take care of business on our end, so we suggest that you take care of yours, or perhaps we should take care of it ourselves, as well as you, the middle one said. So far we have had a wonderful working relationship, but when the stakes are too high we cut our losses, just then the guy from the shadows cut the man hanging from the hook on his back, and another scream came from him. Phillip had no response to the last question, nor any emotion to what was being done, he simply stared straight ahead. Now leave us, as we have unfinished business here one of the men said.

Phillip is escorted out of the room when he hears a deafening scream, the sounds causes his legs to tremble, seeing that, the two guys escorting him away start laughing. Not so tough now are you one said? Phillip was always the one that put the fear into other people and now he got back what he gave. It pissed him off but he was in no position to do anything about it, he just knew he had to stop Jasmine from what she was doing or risk ending up like the guy he saw in the room.

His mind was racing with thoughts as they headed back to the airport, the difference between the ride in and the ride out was that Phillip had no desire to talk to anyone about anything. He arrived at the airport and waited for his flight, he was going to find out today what the hell was going on and stop that bitch before she fucked up everything for him, and he may have to deal with Le'Roi as well, hell he may be the one working with the fed's.

During the flight Phillip went over the scenes in his head as to how he would deal with the situation, no more mister nice guy and if Le'Roi stepped out of line with him he would hand him his nuts. No longer were his thoughts on the reorganization, he was more concerned with saving his ass more so than anything else. Looking at his watch he figured he would not make it back by the end of the work day, so he would head straight home when he landed and get to the bottom of this, as it was now or never.

He never told the other guys exactly who he was working for, the least amount of people that knew anything about the operation was better, especially since some people can't keep their mouths shut. As far as they knew he was the one in charge and he planned to keep it that way. Phillip's plane lands and he immediately heads to his car for the ride home.

His mind was not on anything else other than how to handle his business, even though traffic was heavy due to the end of the workday, he didn't care. Normally he avoided heavy traffic and he didn't like dealing with the assholes that drove erratically, but on this day he just didn't care. When he arrived home he poured himself a drink and waited for Jasmine to come home.

Whatever it was that she knew he was going to find out and put an end to it, as he knew the consequences of his clients losing faith in him and his ability to continue their arrangement.

Chapter 17

On the day of the meeting with Jasmine, he arrived at the room to set everything up and wait for her arrival, he didn't get everything he wanted to but went with what he had anyway. Everything had to be just perfect for her, as this was the kind of affect she had on him and he just couldn't seem to shake the fact that she had him in knots.

While on her way to the meeting, Jasmine felt really good. Phillip was away doing whatever it is he is doing and with the meeting scheduled on the calendar, no one had a need to question her whereabouts. There was only one thing that stuck in her mind, and that was Le'Roi's continued questioning of Phillip and what he might know about their relationship. She had grown quite fond of him and he of her, but it was ticking her off that she felt he didn't have the same confidence in her that she had in him.

Little did she know that while Le'Roi was concerned about Phillip, but more so for his own feelings that he had developed for her. The mere fact that he was going to see her set him off on a frenzy to make sure everything was perfect, this caused more excitement in him now than it did when he first attempted sex. She captivated him with her beauty and her presence lit up any room that she entered.

As the time drew nearer, the more nervous he became and didn't know why. They had been together before and even though it wasn't a full sensual session, they both had seen each other naked so it really wasn't any surprise. Still, the thoughts filled his mind as he wondered how things would be. He checked everything over and over again, wanting the situation to be perfect.

They were a good couple and had fun together doing the simple things; they love to talk to each other on the phone about whatever was on their mind, usually it was about nothing more than life in general. They had been to lunch a couple of times and got to try some very exquisite foods, he took her to a Korean restaurant and she loved Thai food. Although they were seen together in public, nothing could have been said other than they simply had lunch together, which could have easily been explained since they worked in the same company and sometimes had dealings together. What made it even easier was the fact that they were working closely on the reorganization project. That may have been a viable assessment but Le'Roi still felt Jasmine took Phillip not caring for granted and was becoming too comfortable.

He was anxiously awaiting her arrival, and every few minutes he would look out the peep hole or the window for her car, between those checks he would look everything over to make sure nothing was out of order. Finally, she arrived at the meeting place; he opened the door and invited her in. They greeted as she walked by but it wasn't the greeting he was hoping for, still he couldn't help but watch her hips move from side to side as she entered the room.

Her hips moved with the gracefulness of a model, with an attitude that said look but don't touch; her butt looked very inviting with the pants she was wearing. Usually she wore her hair fixed up but today it was pulled back into a pony tail, he figured since she wasn't working there was no need to put it in any special arrangement. For some reason he was nervous as hell, and slyly took a look out of the door to see if anyone was out there, he saw nothing strange and closed the door.

Jasmine put her purse on the table and looked around the room as if to check things out, she looked around as if she expected someone else to be present in the room, when he offered her a seat. His mannerism told her that he was still a bit uneasy and she didn't like that, because she felt that he didn't completely trust her on this. He offered her a drink, she accepted, sat down at the table, and they began their conversation. He was a bit nervous and on edge while she was agitated, he because of Phillip and she because of his lack of trust.

The conversation begins with small talk, but the tension in the room was still thick. Finally, she asked the question that he most feared, "do you trust me or should I leave?" Although he wasn't afraid of the question itself, it was his answer he feared would drive her away. Various thoughts ran through his mind, he finished his drink and poured himself another. I trust you, it is just going to take a bit too fully relax, that's all.

So the question now is she says, is what do you want from me right now?

He looked at her and decided the only thing to do was to tell the truth. Looking in her eyes he said, "I want to be with you and enjoy the moment". As she opened her mouth to speak, he stopped her and said "I really enjoy talking to you and being with you, there are things that I want to do for you but can't offer you anything at this time other than this; I wish I could but we both know that things are difficult at the present and I can't make any promises".

She sat back in the chair and begins to relax, figuring he was thinking something that he wasn't saying. She countered, "So what is it you think that I'm expecting from you or of you?" If it was something material what could you give me that I don't already have? He assured her that wasn't the case, but rather that he was so infatuated with her and filled with the desire to be with her that he felt compelled to ask her over, and take the chance to be with her in spite of the risk involved.

After finishing her drink she got up from the chair, asked for another one, and excused herself to the bathroom, figuring a few moments to ponder the situation will let her know what to do. While she wanted to stay and desired the passion that he ignited within her, his constant questioning and worrying about Phillip made her want to walk away and never speak to him again. He walked behind her and touches her shoulder, as she turned to look at him he takes her in his arms and hugged her, she did nothing. The warmth of her body next to his and the sweet scent of her perfume took him back to the time they first met.

After releasing her she continued to the bathroom. Upon opening the door she was pleasantly surprised. He had a bubble bath waiting for her, with the room lit with scented candles. The aroma filled her nostrils as she stopped to enjoy the smell; this is what she did for her Phillip once and now he were giving it back to her. He replied, "I was hoping that you would like this?" What made you think that I would, she replied? I was just hoping he said. Then she closed the door.

He walks back to the table and noticed that her glass was empty, then realized that she did ask for another drink, he resigned himself to thinking that he blew his opportunity to be with such a gorgeous thing of beauty again because of his insecurities. Not that he was insecure with himself; he just didn't want to cause her any undue drama with Phillip.

He played some music; jazz was what he used to help him relax. His mind begins to wander about what could have been if things had been different, how they seemed to be the perfect couple for each other. He could have kicked himself for being so stupid, as he didn't understand how he could have allowed his feelings to get so deep for her, so deep that he found it hard to walk away. This question he asked himself numerous times, and each time never gave him an answer.

The creaking of the bathroom door brought him from his thoughts and back to the present. He didn't know what to expect, figuring she could either come out and leave without saying a word, and then perhaps she could stay and enjoy the time they planned to spend together. He was a bit surprised and elated when she said "no sense in wasting a good bubble bath", this was the chance he needed he reasoned as a smile came over his face. Besides, she had her own agenda because she was horny and wanted some relief. Although he was delighted, he tried very hard not to show his enthusiasm, as he stood there looking at her. He watched as she slowly began to unbutton her blouse, until she reached the last one. His manhood begins to become aroused as she slid her pants down over her hips and off her legs. As she stood there he couldn't help but remember just how beautiful she was and he had become to love her so.

He walked behind her and hugs her from behind, pressing his now fully hard dick against her butt wondering if he'll ever get the chance to get in it, before he leans back and unfastens her bra, seeing her round breasts as he slid the bra over her shoulders made him want to burst out of his pants. He had to be careful and not move too soon; as he now felt he had a second chance. He reached for her panties and she stopped him there. I'll take it from here she said, and went into the bathroom.

He turned the music up a little louder so that she could hear it, and let the sweet soulful sounds of jazz fill the room. Realizing she left her drink on the table, he decided to take it to her. There she was, a lovely thing of beauty sitting there in the glow of the candles with bubbles all around. It was a picturesque scene that could never be captured again in a thousand years. I thought you might want this he said, and handed her the drink. Coyly she smiled at him. He sat on the edge of the tub and begins to move his hand around in the bubbles, daring to take a chance and feel the warm water against her soft skin. Yes they were comfortable and familiar with each other, but he still respected her and didn't take her for granted.

He started with her toes and begins working his way up her legs, pausing at the knee joints to massage the back of them. He circled her navel and went down the other leg, being careful to not appear anxious and to duplicate his same efforts as on the other leg. He cups a hand of water and poured it over her shoulders, moving some of the bubbles and exposing a nipple. The firmness told him that she was aroused by his touch, letting him know that at least he turned her on, at least he hoped. I'll meet you in the next room he said as he kissed her on the forehead and left the bathroom.

When he departed the bathroom she sighed with relief, his hands on her body caused her to become aroused and even though she was in the bubble bath, she knew that she was wet from his touch and not the water. Her anger had ceased by now and she realized that she had not even kissed him, she wanted him badly but not if he wasn't going to trust her with this situation. They both had a lot to lose and she had even more, so if she was content with the situation why couldn't he she reasoned.

After completing her bath, she wrapped herself in a towel and entered the room. He was lying on the bed wearing a tank top and some shorts, with a bottle of warming oil next to him. He got up and walked over to her, and gently took the towel off. Seeing her there naked just drove him crazy. Lie down on the bed on your stomach he said, she obliged. She lay on her stomach and he gently massaged her neck and shoulders with the warm oil.

Wanting to take his time, he purposely made it his desire to not rush anything as a moment like this was to be treasured. Carefully rubbing warming oil on her body was a dream come true, especially when he reached her buttocks. The nice curvatures of her cheeks made him highly aroused, hell hard as a rock! He had to hide it and not appear too anxious, as he wanted this to last as long as possible, while not rushed like the first time.

Trying to maintain his thoughts, he quietly whispered for her to relax. He took the oil and poured some on her belly, being careful to only touch the spots he wanted at that time. He rubbed her legs with oil and massaged them, all the way down to her toes and back up again. She then realized that she'd forgotten how much she missed his touch. He turns her over and after finishing the backside of her body he whispers "turn over please", which she does.

He moved toward her head and dripped oil onto her chest; the warm oil made sensations run through her body and caused an excitement to stir within her. He was also aroused as the both of them tried to maintain control of the passion that was waiting to be released and not seem too eager, but wanting to play the situation out to the end. The afternoon meeting was good so far, but not yet complete.

Rubbing both breasts with oil, he played with her nipples. Touching, teasing, and squeezing them just to make them hard. The feel of her hard nipples between his fingers and the palm of his hand when he covered her breasts delighted him, and then he moved his hand down to her groin area. He loved the way she kept her box neatly manicured with just a twinge of hair. Sliding his hands between her thighs, he enjoyed feeling the warmness of her and knew that she was ready for him, but not yet.

He rubbed his fingers on the outside of her lips before coming up to circle her clit, this sensation caused her lips to swell and her juices flow more, making her wetter. Slowly he slid a finger between her lips and let it glide over her wetness, which caused her to moan slightly. He watched her facial expressions, which told him that she liked his touch there as her mouth exhibited the most soothing of sounds.

He thought about how good she felt the first time they were together, he wasn't prepared for what happened that day and he also had to get back to work. That made their first time incomplete but now that they had another opportunity and no one having to rush back anywhere, perhaps this time would be different, but then again . . . .

Chapter 18

As he touched her in seemingly all of the right places, thoughts raced through her head. She didn't know whether she should stop him now or let him continue, while she was enjoying his touch on her body, that small voice in the back of her head still wondered if he would trust her and forget about Phillip. Not wanting to ruin the moment she pushed those thoughts out of her head and focused on Le'Roi and how he would make her laugh, and knew just what to do to make her feel special.

His uncanny ability to listen to her whenever they talked and even be able to repeat back those same conversations to her later, showed her that he was sincere in his dealings with her, well as least he was listening to her and that was more than she had received from a man in a very long time.

Thoughts drifted into the first time they made love, when she hastily put her plan together. She was the dominant one the first time they were intimate but during the second encounter that day he proved to be a clumsy sort who thought he knew how to please a woman. Jasmine just didn't have the heart to tell him otherwise, but decided from that day on she would guide him to the right places that gave her pleasure. She also chalked it up to the fact that he did have to get back to work and may have been rushed for time, but today there is no excuse.

There were things that she wanted but didn't want to come straight out and tell him, yes she thought, I will guide him to what I like. Still the concern of him appearing to not trust her and focus on Phillip made her begin to have second thoughts about being with him at that moment, she was confused as she wanted him but not at the expense of trust.

A sensual touch brought her out of her reminiscing and back into the present, he definitely had learned how to touch and please her, not sure what to think but maybe he was indeed not showing all of his cards the first time as this was more to her liking. The way he was touching her almost seemed as if he had just read her mind, perhaps he wasn't as inexperienced as she thought and perhaps she just needed to wait and see how things played out.

Still, she was uncertain as to whether she should continue or stop him, her mind was giving confusing signals and the decision would be easy if only his touch didn't feel so damn good. The way his tongue would barely touch the surface of her body, causing her to have tingling sensations all over. She figured he learned this trick from somebody or somewhere and it felt so good that it sent a fire through her body that she hadn't felt with anybody else, not even her husband Phillip when they were so into each other, certainly he was special to her for that and always would be. But what about afterwards, could they possibly continue to see each other if he had doubts and a lack of trust? Maybe he is really sincere about his paranoia and she simply needs to give him a chance to see where it goes from here?

Before another thought could enter her mind, he did it; he hit the one spot that sent her over the edge. She hadn't noticed but he had taken an ice cube from the bucket and begins rubbing it all over her body. He started at her forehead before slowly moving down to her neck, the coolness of the ice caused her to shiver but still it felt very good to her. He was as considerate as he was passionate, she noticed this when she saw that he kept a towel nearby to catch the falling water as it melted from her warm skin. Moving down to the breasts, he grabbed another piece of ice and started encircling her nipples with it, then putting his mouth and sucking on them.

The hot and cold feeling made her even moister than she had been before, whenever she was truly aroused the flood gates in her pussy would open and her juices would flow freely, sometimes to the point of embarrassment. It had been a very long time since she felt that kind of embarrassment and she was hoping that he wouldn't notice just how wet she really was. She felt the water move down her body as he was working his way down to her navel. She wanted to open her eyes but the feeling felt so good that she didn't want to ruin the moment, she was truly aroused and didn't want to lose the wonderful sensations that she was feeling.

He spread her legs open a bit more and rubbed some more ice on her inner thighs, it was such a sensitive spot for her, almost as sensitive as her clitoris. Perhaps he knew more than she thought he did as he was continuing to amaze her with what he was doing. Shivers went to her head as he did the ultimate, putting the ice cube on her clit and rubbing it all around the inside and outside of her lips. Her clit became highly aroused and swollen as it filled with blood, the cold and wet sensation was causing trembles throughout her body and she enjoyed every sensation that she was experiencing.

Any thoughts that she had about being confused and leaving were well gone by this point, in fact she wasn't even thinking at this point. The cold water dripped down between her cheeks and onto her anus, causing a strange sensation she hadn't felt before, it was almost frightening to the point that she opened her eyes and stared at the ceiling. She remembered how he told her the way he would have anal sex with her and while the thought of it excited her, it also frightened her as she wasn't sure that she was quite ready for the experience. Think she thought, and reminded herself to relax and enjoy the moment, eventually she did but only after she came so close to an orgasm, but lost it because she was letting her mind wander off and not truly focus on the pleasures he was providing.

Suddenly she felt his tongue sliding between her lips as it moved against the moistness of her love box. She loved the feeling it gave her, especially when his hot breath blew on her pussy, why couldn't more men do this she thought. She definitely didn't get this at home and longed for the time when she would be eaten again. Men loved to get their dick sucked but rarely would one want to go down and give the woman pleasure, she loved oral sex and it seemed to make the sexual encounter and intimacy better.

As he was working his magic below, she wanted more and she slowly opened her legs wider to allow him better access, sensing her pleasure he took full advantage of it. The feel of his tongue darting in and out of her hole and around her clit made her feel so good. He had a way of licking her while playing with her breasts that made her want more. She opened her eyes and looked at him, he seemed to be enjoying what he was doing very much, and she liked the fact that he did. There was no way she was going to stop him, hell he could keep going all afternoon if he wanted to she thought.

Watching him and feeling his mouth and hands all over her body was like watching an artist at work trying to create a masterpiece, yes, he was very skilled at his art. She was wondering how he learned such skills when at that moment the movement of his tongue caused a sensation to well within her and she placed her hands on his head to make him get in closer, also so she could lead him to the places she wanted him to go.

She was so wet that she could feel the towel beneath her getting wet from her flowing juices. Perhaps he thought that he could lick her dry, if he thought he could then he should be prepared to go all night and she would still be wet, and she was not going to stop him. Then it begins to happen, she trembled and starts moaning, moving her hips to meet the rotations of his mouth. She moved faster and faster, feeling her body climb towards its peak.

He reached down and spread her cheeks; his tongue was everywhere it seemed. Rotating nicely between her bush and the inside of her thighs, his movements caused her breathing to quicken.

Suck my clit she thought as she tried to divert his attention back to it. He took a finger and rubbed it on her anus which was already wet from the juice that flowed freely, the finger felt good as the new experience for her caused the tension to build even more inside her as the feelings were so strong that she just wanted to explode.

His mouth finally made its way back to the spot that was hot and begging for attention. And without a warning, it happened. She placed her hands on his head and tried to push it inside of her, as the feeling was just that good. The orgasm came on so suddenly that it caught her off guard; the intensity of the climax was so strong that he caused her body to cum so hard that she shuddered and swore she saw stars around the room when she opened her eyes.

Knowing that he had achieved his objective, he smiled and begins playing with her, he knew that her clit being swollen from all of the excitement was very sensitive. Knowing that the slightest touch would cause her to jump, he did it anyway, as it was still throbbing from her orgasm. He loved seeing her lose control like that, and in his mind he wondered if he was the only one that could make her cum like that. Not that he wanted to be compared to any of her previous lover's, he just wanted to give her pleasure like she had not experienced before. That's right he thought, a gigantic orgasmic explosion and he wanted her to have one each time they were together, whenever it was!

He slowly made his way up towards the head of the bed, satisfied with what he just accomplished. He reached over and grabbed his drink off the night stand next to the bed; he then took some of his drink and poured a little on her chest, lapping up every drop before it spilled onto the bed. No words were needed to be said at that point and none were to be spoken, the way their bodies reacted to the encounter said it all.

She was surprised to see that he was still dressed. He looked at her and gently kissed her on her precious lips. She reached up to greet his lips and parted them with her tongue. She wanted to tell him thank you but would that be appropriate she thought? She then decided that she wanted more, but then what kind of message would it send to him? She arrived agitated about the trust issue and now she was ready to fuck his brains out, hell she was confused.

The love making session was great but she didn't want to be lulled into another scenario that caused them to be at odds with each other. She reached for him, and hesitated, then continued and said what the hell. He may have trust issues but right now her pussy needed some dick and that was exactly what she was going to get, although they had to sneak around she wondered if they could they continue to just have sex without a commitment. She was unsure but decided to just see where things went from there.

Chapter 19

Le'Roi looked at her with deep passion in his eyes, taking the time to examine every feature on her face. He loved the fullness of her lips, how her eyes seem to glow whenever she looked at him. There was a glow about her that he loved, and even the dark gloomy days would be brightened by her presence. He was entranced over her and had never felt this way about any woman before, it was almost as if he was brain washed and despite his feelings and thoughts about the situation, he was willing to take the chance to be with her at any available moment.

How could things have gotten to the point that they are he thought, he allowed himself to be pulled into someone else's world when it should have been the other way around. Perhaps if he had not given in to his temptations then things wouldn't have progressed to the point where it is today. He must be a fool to be sleeping around with another man's wife, but hell Phillip didn't care about her, but why did he feel that was something he should be concerned about? It wasn't his problem or issue to deal with, but it potentially could be his problem if Phillip ever found out. Maybe this was their destiny? We all meet people for some reason and perhaps they were meant to be together, but how could that be if she was married. Maybe the best thing for him to do was to get up and leave all of this behind him, but could he really do that? Hell no he thought, and leaned forward and kissed her passionately on the lips.

His kissing her on the lips felt so good, her body had stopped shaking from the intense orgasm he gave her and right now she wanted to do anything to please him the way he had just pleased her. Besides, she still wanted to feel his swollen member deep inside of her. She reached down and rubbed his manhood through the shorts he was wearing.

Take these off she said,

Why don't you do it for me, he responded while looking at her, scared he asked?

Looking at him with a smile on her face she rises up and leans over him, she places a hand on each side of his hips and he lies there with a shit eating grin on his face, he definitely wasn't nervous now as the confidence he felt welled inside of him. His concerns about pleasing her were gone as the orgasm told him that he had nothing more to prove. She wondered just who he thought he was dealing with, she was not scared of him and if he wasn't careful he may get more than he can handle.

She works his shorts down and as she pulls it past his groin his dick pops out and stands straight up in the air, it may have been a deception but she swears it has grown bigger from the first time she saw it. She stops and playfully takes his member in her hand and puts it in her mouth. She continues with the shorts until they are completely off, he then raises himself off the bed and removes his shirt.

Crawling her way up back up to him at the head of the bed, she kisses him fully on the lips as if she was hungry. Moving to his neck, she kisses it slowly while her hand rubs his chest, which felt very strong and muscular. The way his hair laid down was always a turn on for her, the smoothness of it seemed as if it felt like silk. Her mouth moves down and she licks his nipples and is surprised when he makes a slight jump from it, so she moved to the other one and did it again with the same results from him. She never knew that a man's nipple could be an erogenous spot, for a woman yes, but she never thought that it could happen for a man.

As she continues licking his nipples she reached down and takes him in her hand, he is as hard as a rock and throbbing from the sensation of her tongue on his chest. This is a very different experience from the first time she said to herself, him being so hard made her want him even more, she continues working her tongue down his body when she slowly began stroking his member. He raises his head and sees that she is on her knees with her ass in the air; damn she looks good he thought.

Finally reaching his groin area, she playfully kissed all around his throbbing penis; he was very hard and ready to feel her mouth on him. He wanted to say something but was afraid to do so, as it might cause her to tell him to shut up. Yes, he loved the way she performed oral sex on him during the first encounter, even if it was a brief session. Though he had experienced it many times, he never really enjoyed it until he had it with her, he didn't know if he felt that way from the fact that she was really good or did he desire her so much that it just didn't matter? In his mind she was skilled in what she knew, and he had no qualms about her giving him the sensations that made him feel good. He wondered where she learned to do what she did; he was also smart enough to realize that some questions are better left unasked.

She kissed the tip of his penis and inserted it into her mouth. Finally, he thought to himself. Her tongue begin to flicker all around his head, he loved the feel of her mouth on him. The warm feeling that came over him almost seemed too much to bear at times. He had to be careful and not let himself become too excited, as he didn't to spill his load to quickly, she might want to give him the reputation of being a jackrabbit. It really mattered to him what she thought, and he was careful to watch every little detail. Hell, maybe that was his problem.

He looked down at her as she engulfed his entire member into her mouth; damn it felt good to him. She begins to move her head up and down while simultaneously playing with his balls. Yes, she was very skilled at what she did and he fully enjoyed the way her tongue would flicker the tip and she would fully engulf his manhood. It was like a repetition that constantly repeated itself in rhythmic fashion. She sucked him until he raised his head up and asked her to stop.

She laughed and said "what's the matter, too hot for you?"

No, I am ready to get deep inside of you before I explode was his reply.

He reached over into the drawer on the night stand and got a condom, after putting it on he pulls her up to him and she straddles herself on top. He liked this position as it gave him full access to her rounded breasts. In spite of everything else he liked, he was a breast man who loved to be fed so to speak. He slowly entered her and felt her lips enclosed on him, it felt so good to be with her again. He begins with small thrusts, and begins to work his way up to more forceful ones. She closed her eyes and enjoyed the feeling of him inside of her. Feeling his thrusts, she begins to match him one for one. Rolling her hips to his every move, causing her to pant and moan at the sensation.

The bouncing of her breasts in his hands filled him with even more excitement. He knew he had to be careful otherwise he may cum too early and that would be the one thing he didn't want. He allowed his mind to drift to other things, such as what he had to do, how he met her, or just about anything to keep him going. He also had to be careful and not think too much otherwise he might go soft and that would be just as bad. To be safe he figured he better pay attention to the issue at hand.

He looked at her and a smile came across his face. That's right, her facial expressions told him that he still had her going and by god he was going to work it. What did he have to lose? Nothing he thought, as this very well may be the last time they were together, so he may as well go for broke.

Le'Roi starts raising himself with deep thrusts into Jasmine's wet pussy; the look on her face tells him that she wasn't expecting that but also welcomed it. There was a time to make love with passion and then there are the times where you just want to fuck. A smart person would know how to intermix the two together and today he was going to be that smart person. Let's change positions he said.

Okay, how do you want me she asked?

No darling, how do YOU want it?

I want it from behind on my hands and knees.

No problem, he said.

Le'Roi checked his condom to make sure it was okay, it was. He gets on his knees in between her legs, pushing her legs out with his own before slowly inserting himself inside her. He goes slowly at first to make sure that she is fully ready for all of him, he realizes she is when she starts pushing back against him to meet his every thrust. They both go faster; he spreads her cheeks to allow every inch of his manhood to disappear inside her.

Pull my hair she said, he gently pulls on her ponytail while continuing to stroke her, harder she said, he pulls harder and her rhythm picks up as her moans get louder until she shakes from another orgasm. This is too much for him as he reaches his point and collapses on top of her while continuing to push himself to insert every drop of his semen, she helps him by contracting her muscles while moving up and down to make sure he is empty.

They lay there panting and thinking about how wonderful it was, he is dripping wet with sweat all over her but she doesn't mind, that was the best sex she has had in a long time. The way he was able to move his body and meet her movements told her that he was a treat and desire to have.

He pulls out and checks the condom to make sure it is intact; he then lies next to her. He wants to hold her but right now the two of them are so hot that it wouldn't be any fun at all, each are satisfied with their lovemaking session and although not aware of it, both are wanting more and hoping this isn't the last time they would be together.

The time that they were together flew by way too quickly; they finished their drinks and separately took a shower. He figured one day they would actually make it into the shower, together. There was no need to rush anything as time was on their side, so you may as well save something for later he thought to himself.

Chapter 20

After cleaning up they both departed separately and went in different directions, just in case someone was watching them or ran across them unexpectedly. She left first and when he was on his way out he called her cell and they talked all the way home and only stopped when Jasmine saw Phillip's car parked in the driveway. This was very unusual for him to be home so early in the evening, if at all. He would often leave with no hint or clue as to where he was going or had been when he returned.

Jasmine walked into the house and was immediately grabbed by Phillip, "where the hell you been" he asked? I was just out. Doing what he asked? Just getting some air she replied.

Yeah, you seem to be doing that a lot these days, if you need so much air then maybe you should keep your ass out there he shouted.

Please let me go; you're hurting my arm came her reply. Phillip released his grip on her but she stood frozen by the door, wondering what he was going to do next. He had a habit of putting his hands on her in a physical manner, and although it had been a while since that happened, she still understood his anger and what came along with it.

Phillip walked into the front room and picked his drink from the table and took a swig and yelled out, "what? You scared to come in now"? Jasmine walked past him and went into the kitchen where she put her purse on the counter, cautious to keep her eyes on him. What is wrong with you Phillip?

Why are you treating me like this?

I want to know if you have something that you want to tell me, he said in a stern voice.

Something like what?

Is there something, you want to tell me he asked again, this time more sternly than before.

No, there is nothing to tell, I went out for some air and you are giving me shit about it? Maybe I should do the same thing to you when you go out doing whatever the hell it is that you do?

This isn't about me at the moment and don't try to turn this around on me, came his reply.

Well maybe it should be about you and all the shit that you do and think people doesn't know about she screamed. It was at that point she realized that maybe she had said too much, for a moment they both just stared at each other in total silence, which was only broken when Phillip said "I don't know what the hell you are talking about and right now I am not in the mood to discuss something you may have heard from whom knows where". He picked up his drink and walked into the study.

A sign of relief came over Jasmine as she realized just how close she came to feeling the wrath of Phillip, it has been along time since he hit her and even though he promised to never do it again, she felt as though she had pushed the button that makes him fly into that kind of rage.

Finally she was able to move and went to get a glass of wine, she had just enough for one glass in the open bottle, her hands were still shaking from the encounter and she knew she had to settle her nerves or her really would be suspicious. The strange thing is she doesn't know what caused him to question her like that, what motives did he have, or perhaps what had he heard about her. The relationship with Le'Roi was discreet and she knew he was not the type to brag or boast of his exploits, something was going on and she had to figure out what it was.

While sitting in the study, Phillip's mind was roaming trying to figure out what she had heard, from whom she heard it, and just how much did she know about what he was doing. Only a select few knew what was happening and if anyone talked they all would go down as he was sure one would implicate them all. He had to find out who was talking and things had to be dealt with quickly, time for a meeting he concluded.

He picked up the phone and called a number which a voice answered on the other end, meeting tomorrow at 1 o'clock, no exceptions Phillip said. The voice on the other end said "okay"; I will pass the message for everyone to be there and hung up. Phillip knew he had to get down to the bottom of this and he needed to neutralize the source quickly, there was too much at stake and he was not about to lose what he had or go down alone. He figured the best way to do that was to address the issue head on and see who was cooperating with Jasmine or feeding her information.

Phillip walks into the kitchen and puts his empty glass on the counter and sees the empty wine bottle Jasmine left on the counter, fucking drunk was his thought. To him all she seemed to do was drink and take those damn pills to battle her so-called depression, strangely enough this only happened after work and not during, shit he didn't care as long as she was contributing to the house. He had his fun and he knew where to go to get it, in fact he needed some right now and he was going to get it. He walks into the bedroom and sees that she has already showered and in the bed, he wasn't sure if she was not asleep nor did he particularly care.

His eyes look at the shape under the covers and reflected upon a time when he would desire her so much that he couldn't keep his hands off her. That was when they were younger and he was just starting as an apprentice in the company and didn't know his ass from a hole in the ground, but as he moved up the ladder things came to him freely as it was all a part of the game. Things became so good "the fringe benefits that is" that basically he didn't feel a need or desire to be with Jasmine anymore, but perceptions are everything in the corporate world and his going through a divorce right now would not be looked upon favorably within the corporation, for she was with him when he didn't have anything and to leave her would look like he used her to catapult himself ahead.

There was already the pressure of them dating within the company until they got married, the company didn't want to set a precedent and it was because of them that the no dating policy was developed. Fuck this shit he thought, I have a hot pussy waiting on me. He showered got dressed and left without as much as a word or note to Jasmine.

As she lay there listening to Phillip move around she wanted to say something to him but didn't want to risk another confrontation. She used to get upset that he would leave with no mention of where he was going or when he would return, now it was as if she accepted this fate and was content to just let things go as they did. She wanted to cry and almost did until a thought entered her mind, she got up and retrieved her cell phone from her purse and called the number on speed dial location 7.

Hello came from the voice on the other end, hi baby was her reply. Yes, she knew that calling Le'Roi would always make her feel better; calling this late was outside of the norm but knowing Le'Roi he was never bothered by her calling, no matter what time or day. That is what made him so special, he made her feel alive and she hoped that she did for him what he did for her, he said he was content being with her, but still cautious about being seen. In her mind she was his for as long as he would have her.

What's going on he said, nothing much, Mr. Man just left to go do whatever and I wanted to hear my baby's voice. Oh, okay, nothing wrong with that he said, I really enjoyed myself this evening, and your company is always good, even when we just talk. I feel the same way she said, I just wish that he would treat me with the same respect that you do. Remember our promise, no comparisons. Yes I know she said, but sometimes I just think about it so much.

Try not to, it will only make you resent him more and I don't want to be the cause of any drama in your life. You are not the cause of anything Le'Roi; my problems with Phillip were here long before you came into the picture she said. Believe me Le'Roi said, I have truly enjoyed every moment that I have spent with you, we just have to be careful. Jasmine thought about the situation that occurred tonight, but felt it best not to share it with Le'Roi as that would just make him that much more cautious and she didn't want to risk pushing him away from her.

Look, I hate to be a party pooper but I have an early morning meeting with a perspective client tomorrow morning and the morning will come quickly Le'Roi said. Okay baby, you have a good night and sweet dreams, of me. I hope so he said. Goodnight baby! Goodnight.

Jasmine hung up the phone and lay back on the bed and thought about Le'Roi and how he made her feel emotionally, physically, and mentally. She had never encountered a man that made her feel so desired, even when she and Phillip were getting along well, there was no comparison to what she was feeling right now.

The mere thought of Le'Roi touching her caused her kitty to start singing and longing to be touched. Her hand brushed across her nipples under her teddy, she was aroused and they were hard, begging for some attention. Funny how she was so aroused when she had been satisfied earlier, but this is what Le'Roi did for her, she enjoyed life and he was responsible for it. While she had just gotten her "some" earlier today, her thinking about Le'Roi made her want more.

Her hands squeeze her breasts and pull at her nipples, she closes her eyes and imagines that Le'Roi's hands are touching her breasts, her breath quickens as her sensitive nipples are teased and played with. She slides her right hand down to her belly and pulls her teddy up, exposing her groin area as she opens her legs and keeps going until her hand stops at the kitty, as she touches herself even she is surprised at how wet she is.

The slippery moisture has covered her kitty and makes her fingers slide effortlessly around her passion fruit. She wishes Le'Roi was there to taste her juices and then for him to kiss her so she could have a taste also. Her hand moves from her kitty to her mouth as she sucks the sweet nectar of the juices off her fingers before taking them down for more. Her fingers encircle her clit and moves between her lips, making her juices pour between her cheeks and covering her ass.

Jasmine knew how to please herself but now she was thinking about Le'Roi and how he pleased her, her hands move in a rhythmic motion while she concentrates on Le'Roi. The feeling is overwhelming and spontaneous to the point that she is about to explode, just a little longer and she will have her orgasm. The intensity builds and her nectar is flowing like a river as she reaches the point of orgasm and just as she is about to reach climax, the phone rings and causes her to lose focus.

She continues working her fingers when she climaxes, causing her breathing to become quick and shallow, she tries to but can't really enjoy it because the phone is still ringing. Damn it she screams, looks at the caller ID and sees it is someone she knows, she picks up the phone and says, hi mom . . . .

Chapter 21

The next day at the meeting that Phillip called, everyone is seated in the conference room awaiting his arrival. He comes in and says "I want a progress report by the end of the day on the reorganization", the people in the room gasp as this was unusual to get a such a major request like this on short notice.

Is there any particular reason why it has to be today someone asked?

Yes, I want to make sure that you all are focused on what you should be doing and not being distracted by other things or events, Phillip said.

What other things, Le'Roi asked? I believe that we all have been properly focused on the reorganization and the other issues that may arise.

Okay, since you want an example I'll give you one, how about the Zylander Company. The finance department needs financial statements to reconcile the reports and there doesn't appear to be much information available on them, so if anyone has that information or know where I can find it I will personally handle it. I don't want them to fall behind on accomplishing their task and since the information may be needed from all of you it could prove to be a distracter. That will free you all up to concentrate on what you need to be during for the reorganization.

In her mind Jasmine was wondering why Phillip took such an avid interest in this case, he was never the one to do hands on type work and this was certainly out of his realm. What made this so important that he was willing to do layman's work? Her mind was preoccupied with her own thoughts of Phillip and Zylander when she heard him say "oh and Jasmine, I need you to go back to Atlanta for a few days. There something I need to you to look over and resolve.

But there's sufficient expertise back there, what could possibly be so important that it requires my personal attention, she asked?

Phillip was beginning to become angry as he felt that his authority was being questioned and challenged. Because "I" made the decision that you would do it and that decision is final! He made it a point to emphasize the he was the one who made that decision, he wanted to make it known that he was calling the shots and it left no doubt in anyone's mind that he was in charge, because if he treated his own wife like that in public each knew that they would get worse.

You leave tomorrow he said. Lastly, I want those progress reports today, no exceptions and definitely no excuses! Phillip leaves the room and everyone looks at each other, there was no need to complain about it as what good would it do? Finally one person got up and eventually everyone departed the room and set out to fulfill the request.

Le'Roi went with Jasmine back to her office and stared at her while leaning against the wall, he wasn't sure what to say so he just looked at her. She was upset and there was nothing that he could do to comfort her, especially being in the workplace.

I'll call you when I get there she said.

Okay, hey if you need something from here let me know.

I'll only be gone for a few days so what would I possibly need?

I'm just saying whatever it is I have your back.

I want to see you when I get back she said.

Let's take it from that point when we get there, I don't want to be too hasty with our planning and we shouldn't be discussing this here, you never know who is listening. Let me go and work on my report, I'll talk with you later.

Okay, later.

Phillip's plan to send Jasmine back to Atlanta had a dual purpose, he could go through her files in the office and email to see what she had done or found out, the second part of that was his guys would be able to follow her to see if she was talking to someone about Zylander.

Jasmine arrived back in Atlanta and found a stack of papers on her desk, the note attached said they were to be reviewed for accuracy. When Jasmine asked who put the papers on her desk, the secretary told her that Phillip personally wanted her to review the papers for financial accuracy, sort of a verification process. This was not her kind of work and was usually done by someone not in her position. As she was looking at the stack of papers the president of the Atlanta office came down to greet her.

Welcome back Jasmine, even if it is just for a few days he said.

I'm not sure why I was brought back for this sir but we'll see what is going on.

I spoke to Phillip and he told me about some accounting irregularities and he felt that you were the only one he could trust to verify them. The last thing we need is an SEC investigation, as our shareholders wouldn't like it. That's why he and I agreed you were the right person for the job.

I understand sir. I'll make sure this is thoroughly followed through. Jasmine's discontent for doing the job was running throughout her body, but she didn't want to give the impression and show her unhappiness.

I know you will so take as much time as you need, and thank you Jasmine for doing this for us.

Yes sir.

When the president departed, Jasmine sat down and wondered why Phillip just didn't say that at the meeting. Maybe he was on the level and is trying to find out about Zylander? Jasmine was unsure about this as usually Phillip always had a motive for the things he did, but what was it this time?

On the second day of her return to Atlanta, all of the transactions that she went through seemed legitimate, there were a couple of misplaced entries but nothing so major as to warrant an SEC investigation. She was bored and decided to send an email to Le'Roi; she missed him and wanted to feel his arms around her. Hey sexy the email said, call me later!

About twenty minutes later her phone on the desk ranged, hello, hey what's up said the voice on the other end?

Nothing, just wanted to hear your voice.

How's the validation process going?

I didn't ask you to call me to talk about work now did I?

So what do you want to talk about?

You know?

Look Jasmine I am really busy, mind telling me what you want he screamed.

It was that moment that she realized she had made a mistake, looking back at her sent folder, she sees that the email that she had sent mistakenly went to Phillip and not Le'Roi as she had intended. Damn it she thought to herself.

She had to think quickly so as to not arouse suspicion; I just thought that you wanted to talk since I hadn't spoken to you since I left.

Bullshit he thought to himself, that message was meant for someone else, but who? Sorry about snapping at you like that, I was just reading the progress reports and trying to make sure we are still on track for the reorganization.

Well since you are busy I'll talk with you later.

Okay, if I get a chance I'll call you back he said, knowing full well that he wasn't going to do so.

Jasmine also knew that he was not going to call her back, but the lesson that she just learned gave credibility to Le'Roi's concern about her slipping up. What if Phillip didn't believe her, maybe he did but if he didn't he might start to check up on her. She picked up her cell phone and called Le'Roi, hello?

Hey, I really need to talk with you she said

Let me go someplace and I'll call you back, where are you?

I'm in my office right now.

I need you to go someplace where you can talk, privately away from the office he told her.

Okay.

I will hit you back in a few minutes.

Ten minutes later he called her back and she explained the mix up with the email, did you mention my name?

No I didn't.

Did you say anything that could have given him the possibility of who you were intending to send that message to?

No.

Then I wouldn't say anything about it unless he brought it up again, but you have to tell the same story otherwise he will become suspicious.

Why did you use the work email? You have to be more careful.

I just wasn't thinking but it won't happen again.

Use my other email address, but don't do it from work.

When Jasmine was walking back to her office Tom was standing inside the doorway, what are you doing she asked? Tom turned around startled and she saw that James was in her office by the desk.

What's going on, and why are you in my office she said.

Nothing James said, I was just looking for some ideas on rearranging some offices and I was impressed by your setup.

Well if you don't mind, I'd appreciate it if you could admire it from the door.

That's fine, we were just about to leave anyway, didn't mean any harm.

As they departed Jasmine became a bit suspicious, there was ample opportunity to view her office while she was away in Columbia so why now is it so important that they look at the arrangement of her office?

Chapter 22

When Le'Roi had finished his conversation with Jasmine he went back inside and saw that Phillip was standing in the lobby, hey bro where you been he asked?

Out talking with a potential client.

Any good news?

No, couldn't close the deal, but I think I'm close.

Tell me who it is and I'll see what I can do to help.

That's okay, I have this Le'Roi said

Hey man we all need a little help sometimes

True, and I appreciate your offer but I'm cool with this

Alright but remember this, you never shit where you eat!

What do you mean by that?

It will come in due time, just remember my words of wisdom to you.

If you have something to say then say it, Le'Roi replied . . .

Look you little shit, I will say whatever the fuck I want to say, whenever I want to say it, and to whomever I want to say it.

Then I suggest . . . .

Gentlemen how is it going today were the words coming from the executive vice president. Business is looking good and I have my two best people having a disagreement in the lobby, resolve this behind closed doors and do it now.

It's all done sir Phillip said, no more discussion is necessary.

Good, now let's do what we should be doing.

Good thing the V.P. came through when he did Le'Roi thought, he didn't want a confrontation but he was damned if he would let Phillip treat him like one of his henchmen. Still the words that Phillip spoke to him bothered him, and what did he mean by that statement. He settled into his office and saw he had a text message from Jasmine thanking him for the discussion today. He figured he better speak to her later about what happened, he didn't want to do it then because he had no privacy.

Later that evening Le'Roi called Jasmine on her phone and he tells her about the encounter with Phillip in the lobby and asks if he knew she called him today? Of course not she replied, why the hell would I do that?

Maybe it is just a coincidence that he was waiting in the lobby but we shouldn't use company email as a means of communications, since it can be monitored.

Okay, but I won't make that mistake again she said.

They continued their conversation and it eventually lead to the topic of sex. Did you enjoy yourself the last time we were together she asked?

Yes, I enjoyed myself very much, even though you didn't get the full repertoire of my skills. In due time you might get to experience the full effect of what I have to offer, that is, if we continue to progress toward that level, he responded.

Feeling sarcastic she replied with "maybe all I want is a friendship and nothing more. What made you think I wanted to go that route; maybe you were just an afternoon delight for my pleasure".

She couldn't see it but a stunned look came over his face and he remained quiet. It seemed to give her pleasure saying things like that as if to show that she was in control. Le'Roi again questions how he let himself get so involved with her.

Laughter interrupted his thoughts as she replied "I was just kidding", I am not the kind of woman that just fucks somebody and then move on. Damn man, you take stuff too seriously sometimes, you need to learn how to relax and have some fun. Just for the record I want you to know that it's either you or no one, and frankly darling you are it. They continued talking for almost an hour. Later that night he received a text message on his phone with the words "hugs and kisses", which he replied "back at you".

Jasmine had now been gone over two weeks and neither was sure when she would return to Columbia, the good part was that it gave them an opportunity to talk frequently without having to sneak around. Over the past few weeks he got to know a lot more about her, it was just amazing to him how well they could just talk on the phone for hours about anything and everything and never tire of the conversation.

Both of them found it easy to talk to the other person and sometimes the conversation moved into the sexual arena, as they discussed things they wanted to do to each other and what they had experienced and wanted to do. He was surprised to learn that she had never tried anal sex before; of course this caused a desire in him to swell as he wanted to be the one to experience it with her. Although she never told him, she liked the way he played with her butt as it added a level of excitement with her. Yes, one day they will have to try it but no rushing, as she was curious about it but also leery doing it.

One day Jasmine went into the office and found a package sitting outside of her door, it had her name on it but no indication of whom it came from. She took the package and placed it on her desk as she settled in, she didn't want to open it but curiosity was getting the best of her so she did. Inside were paper transactions on the Zylander Company, as she continued to go through them it hit her, these are the missing files!

The shock of these documents in her hands caused her to throw caution to the wind as she picked up the phone and called Le'Roi, he wasn't in yet and instead of leaving a message she decided to send him an email, making sure that it was he that she sent the message to. I have some information on Zylander; call me when you get this the email said. As she continued looking through the papers she realized that they were back as far as three years, but why were they taken out of the system she wondered? These papers were the only proof of the transactions as no electronic information was available.

Jasmine then realized that she had to go through the entire box before she said anything to anyone; she also realized that she shouldn't have sent the email to Le'Roi, what if someone read his email and realized what she had? There really was nothing to hide from her perspective but the way Phillip was so interested in this company made her all the more suspicious, as he had never gotten into that level of work since he became an executive.

She put all of the papers into the box and resealed it with tape, she bent down to place the box under her desk and she received another shock, taped under her desk was some type of electronic device, what is this she said out loud? When she did that the device turned on and started recording, she took it down and saw that it was a voice activated recorder. Her mind started going in all different directions and wondered why someone would place that in her office under her desk, then she remembered the day Tom and James were at her office.

Perhaps they did this, but why? Jasmine stopped the tape, rewound it and listened to the conversation that was on it. The recording was of all her conversations she had in the office, even the times when she talked to herself. Then she heard a piece to the puzzle, the tape had the conversation of her calling Le'Roi and the time he told her to go outside to talk to him. Then it dawned on her, maybe Phillip has this done and that's why he was waiting in the lobby for Le'Roi that day, the tape recording only had her on it so there was no way he could have known that it was Le'Roi she was talking to. All kinds of theories came into play but she had no conclusive evidence to tie any of it all together, she had to talk to Le'Roi about this and figure out how to proceed.

She fast forwarded the tape to the last part and put the recorder back in place to appear as if it hadn't been touched, she also knew that she had to be cautious about her conversations since she knew someone wanted to know what she was talking about and to whom, but why?

About an hour later James comes at her door and asks if she found out anything on the Zylander Company? No I haven't she said, I have been busy with the review of these old financial transactions and besides, Phillip is handling everything with Zylander.

Okay, thanks he said and then departed.

Now why would he suddenly come out the blue and ask that question she wondered, that's it, she needed Le'Roi and she needed him now!

Chapter 23

Things went pretty well that week for Le'Roi, he spoke with Jasmine almost daily and it seemed that he was always more energetic whenever he spoke to her, but now it was back to work. For some reason this week got off to a good start, everyone seemed to be overly kind to him and he didn't understand why, usually it was he who always gave the first greeting but now people were speaking to him first. He didn't understand it but saw no reason to question it, it was later that he would learn that his newfound respect came from standing up to Phillip in the lobby. Many people have always wanted to do that but no one had the nerve or guts to do it until Le'Roi did it, which seemed to energize the rest of the workforce.

Le'Roi was no hero nor was he an organizer of anything, he was content to do what he did and he thought he did it well. There was no way he was getting involved in any kind of rebellion, either formal or informal in an effort to do whatever to Phillip. That's it; he needed to get back to his routine of working out as he had dismissed that portion of his life since getting to know Jasmine on a more personal level. He found that his frustration level was increasing; this was due to the lack of exercise or being horny.

Le'Roi knew that he was missing a part of himself, not that he really minded, but exercise was his sanity check, as he loved to work out and he saw exercise as his passion. He would start the day early when most people wouldn't even think about rolling over in bed, let alone getting up and going for a run or doing something productive. Yes sometimes even he thought he was crazy for getting up early, especially on a day off during the weekend but it was his passion and he loved it.

There were even jokes among his co-workers at the office in Columbia that maybe he was using exercise as an excuse for not dating, but their words never bothered him because if they only knew the truth, but then again, some things are better left unsaid. He just took it in stride and laughed along with them as he never needed anyone to define who he was as a man. He loved looking at the ladies in the gym, yes some were cute and he always seems to find something unique about each of them individually.

His workout time was strictly business for him and it was something he took very seriously, still he couldn't resist the temptations of looking at a sweaty woman with hard nipples that protruded under her over garment, they seem to encourage him to work out harder or show off a little bit more than usual, as having a woman with hard nipples were his delight. Yes, a little perkiness never hurt anyone was what he was thinking. Now that Jasmine was away, he needed to get back into his routine since his "distraction" wasn't there.

The next day he was getting his swoll-on as he would often say; which was his term for getting his weight workout and pumping his muscles up to full strength, when a young lady stopped by and gave him a compliment on his workout program. Initially he dismissed it as friendly conversation, but as it progressed he found out that she had been watching him previously when he was in the club. She knew that he hadn't been there in a couple of weeks but always looked for him whenever she came in, as per her statement. This piqued his interest and he wondered what her motive was? After a few minutes she left and he got back to doing his thing, getting his swoll-on.

He saw her again the next day and for once he looked at her and realized just how beautiful she was. Her hair was medium length that complimented her face, but what won him over was her personality. Okay, she had a banging body too but what the heck. Looks are cool but if baby ain't got nothing upstairs then don't waste your time; he didn't need any drama in his quiet life. Finally he asked her name and found it was Colleen, eventually the conversation got to a point where she asked him out, she seemed rather surprised he accepted, they exchanged telephone numbers and agreed to call each other.

The first date wasn't anything special, just some dinner and conversation. He didn't do the club scene and luckily she didn't either. A nice quiet mellow jazz club was the more likely choice. As the evening came to a close her walked her to the door and kissed her on the cheek. Although she didn't mind, she would have preferred a kiss on the lips instead of her cheek, but she respected him for being a total gentleman that evening.

Thursday was coming up and he was supposed to call Jasmine that evening but he didn't because he wanted to see what opportunity he might have with the young lady from the health club. Jasmine was good but he realistically knew that he didn't have a future with her, as long as she was married to Phillip, and he didn't want to let a potential opportunity pass him by.

Jasmine called Le'Roi to inform him of what she had been given, when she couldn't reach him she became upset and wondered what the hell he was doing that prevented him from talking to her. Since they had been together, she was always able to call him and they talk, but lately it seemed that he was never available when she needed him. She basically thought of him as hers, even though he really wasn't hers. She had to get back and see what the hell was going on, as she hadn't realized that she was possessive of him and the mere thought of him being with someone else didn't sit well with her at all.

Several more days had passed and Le'Roi and Colleen seem to hit it off pretty well. He still spoke with Jasmine on almost a daily basis but would always call his new friend shortly either before or after he spoke with Jasmine. He liked taking the time to send Colleen little gifts, not as a means of trying to buy her, but because it was something that he liked to do. Colleen seemed very appreciative and didn't require a lot out of him as she was content to let him do his thing. The biggest hang up was the fact that it seemed he was always the one to initiate the conversations, he understood this was the old way of thinking and figured that if a woman was attracted to him then she should be able to talk to him, just like she did in the health club.

One thing that he couldn't stand a begging woman and whatever he did for her was out of no obligation, just generosity that was strictly from the heart, as it gave him just as much pleasure to give to her as it was for her to receive the gift from him. They sent flirtatious chat messages to each other and sometimes the conversation even was of a sexual nature, hell that's what grown people do he thought.

As he talked with Colleen more and more, he found that Jasmine was becoming less of the center of attention in his life. Sometimes he even felt a little guilty about it, but why he asked himself? Jasmine was committed and although he said he would never get involved with a woman that was attached, he did. While he felt no allegiance to Jasmine, he was very excited about the prospects of what type of a future could be held with Colleen. What was it about Colleen that made him put Jasmine on the back burner? He didn't know but definitely wanted to find out.

One day Colleen called him and invited him to dinner at her house, she had planned to cook and then figured they would watch some movies. Initially he was shocked but this is what he was wanting so it shouldn't have come as a surprise to him. He accepted the invitation and looked forward to the evening. He arrived at her house with a bottle of wine, he didn't know what the meal consisted of but he figured red wine would go with just about anything, at least he had the decency to have it at serving temperature when he gave it to her.

Walking in he admired her house, not that he was inspecting it, but it was a nice cozy setting with everything in its proper place. He wasn't a neat freak, but also believed that you shouldn't have to move back clothes from the door to get in. He settled in and she offered him a drink, a shot of cognac with an ice cube was his choice. He was surprised when she returned with two drinks; she was curious about the cognac that way and wanted to know what it was like. She tried and thought “it’s okay”. Come on, let’s go eat she said.

Dinner consisted of some damn good pot roast, potatoes, carrots and man was it good. He had not had that type of cooking in a very long time, and the wine he brought was perfect with the meal. She put her foot, legs, and booty into that meal he thought to himself, this was key for him as he didn’t want a microwave woman. A microwave woman is someone that could only cook things in the microwave. Doing the proper thing, he let her know just how much he appreciated her cooking the meal, and even made her smile when he asked if he could have seconds. After his second portion was finished and his belly was stuffed to the maximum, she asked if he wanted something sweet for dessert.

Yeah, you were his thoughts, but instead he replied that he was too full for dessert. Just out of curiosity, what is dessert he asked? Freshly made chocolate cake with ice cream? I don’t know how you found the time to make all of this tonight but I am very appreciative of the fact that you did all of this for our date, while the dessert sounds good, I am so stuffed I think I may burst, maybe later, he said.

The choice of movies was drama, horror, or some girly flick that women want a man to watch to see how they react. Nice try he thought, being the typical guy he chose the drama. The movie was okay, but somehow they just don’t make them that intellectually challenging like they did in the past. The movie went on and the plot was figured out early, it was just a matter or how they would arrive to it.

Next up was the horror movie, anything to stay away from the girly stuff. Horror movies kind of make me scared she said. Don’t worry he replied, I’ll be here to protect you from the monster as he let out a little laugh. He couldn’t help but smile to stifle the laughter that wanted to explode from his body, as he thought that she was putting him on. When he realized that she didn’t find it amusing, his smile quickly went away. Taking a more serious tone, he asked did she want to watch the other movie. No this is fine she said, he could have jumped and hit the ceiling, for she had saved the day so to speak. He didn't have to worry about watching a man hating girly movie and after this movie was over, he would leave.

As the movie started, he turned down the lights to have a more dramatic affect. He noticed that she had taken her shoes off and was curling up on one end of the couch. Should I turn the lights back up he asked? No, she said. The movie progressed and she was handling it pretty well, when suddenly the scene changed and she jumped. He looked at her and then realized that she really was afraid, so he turned the light back on. Feeling bad that he had even suggested the movie, he moved toward her as a sign of reassurance and took her hand to comfort her.

Wait a minute he thought, what am I doing? He didn't know what his feelings were at that point even though he knew where he wanted to go, but what was her intentions and how would she receive his actions? Le'Roi wasn't sure but figured that he'll see where the situation progresses from there.

During another scene she jumped again, he figured that he had better do something so he put his arm around her shoulders. To his surprise she laid her head on his chest. She smelled really good. Not that he was hoping she would smell any different, but she smelled very good. At least she wasn't jumping anymore. Later, he started rubbing her back. It was only when she said how good it felt did her realize he was doing it, and then he stopped. Why did you stop she asked? Sorry, I didn't realize I was doing that came his reply. Well don't stop now; keep going she said.

Suddenly, the movie didn't seem as interesting as she did. Wondering if he should try to take it to the next level, he looked at her for some type of signal, but wouldn't be sure if she sent one or not since he really didn't know her that well. He loved the way her body felt when rubbing it, and his mind drifted to other things when he started getting an erection. He tried to think of other things like cars, the job, sports, anything to keep him from getting a hard-on. It didn't work. He even tried pushing his butt down into the couch to keep her from noticing or inadvertently hitting him there and finding out that he was aroused.

Daring to take a chance, he rubbed her hair and titled her head back and gently kissed her on the forehead. She seemed to like it so he did it again; this time he let his hand brush ever so lightly against the side of her breast. This caused her to let out a soft moan, this was a sign of encouragement for him and he leaned her back and kissed her on the lips when her tongue darted into his mouth. Surprised at first, he then slides his tongue across hers and let his hands roam on her breasts. He could feel the arousal of her nipples through her clothes and that caused him to become even more excited.

Chapter 24

By now the movie was a foregone conclusion of being uninteresting to the both of them. He undid a couple of buttons on her blouse and exposed her bra, her smooth skin felt like velvet to his hand as he worked his way up to her breasts and slid them from under her bra. Wait a minute she said, as she sat up and reached around and unfastened her bra so it didn't strain against her chest. There, that's better, now where were we? He started kissing her again, paying close attention to how well it felt to kiss her, and why it took him so long to do it. Her soft lips pressing against his were as soft as a pillow, while he loved sliding his tongue ever so slowly into her mouth and over her slippery tongue. This was good, but he didn't want to neglect her exposed breasts.

Kissing her neck, he slowly moved down to his favorite part of a woman's body, the breasts! His mouth paused momentarily in front of her right nipple when he leaned back to get a view. Her breast looked so lovely, nice and round. Some people loved size, but to him it wasn't about size, for a hard nipple did more for him than anything else. Gently he covered his mouth on her nipple, taking the time to feel the firmness in his mouth.

They aren't going to break you know, she whispered.

Taking a cue, he sucked harder and gently nibbled on her nipple. Her sighs told him that he was doing the right thing; she liked a little roughness on her nipples. At this point he felt there was no need to neglect the other one as his mouth moved to her left nipple and repeated the act. He slid down between her legs and grabbed both breasts with his hands, and carefully paid attention to each one for fear of making the other being jealous. That was his joke to himself because he loved the breasts.

Time to take this to another level he thought; let's go to the bedroom he said, she agreed and led him to it. When they got to the bedroom they both kissed each other and started undressing when he stopped her, no he said, let me do this. He begin by finishing unbuttoning her blouse and removing it off her shoulders, her perky nipples stood out from under the bra that covered the top of her breasts. She removed the bra to expose her lovely assets; they looked even more beautiful in the bedroom light. He removed his top and pants while she watched; the juices begin flowing in her body as she liked what she saw. Yes she was wet and ready for some action, but there was no way that she was going to go down on him until he went down on her first. Most men liked to be done but didn't want to return the favor; this way if he doesn't do her, then she doesn't do him. Little did she know that would be the one thing she wouldn't have to worry about, as she was ready to give as good as she got from him.

After unbuttoning her pants, he had her lie on the bed face down so that he could remove her pants. He was pleasantly surprised when he saw the she was wearing a thong, his second favorite thing on a woman. Her round buttocks looked nice in the thong as he thought about all of the things he would like to do to it, he put his mouth on her cheeks and kissed them passionately. His tongue was hungry but it wasn't feeding time just yet. As she lay on her stomach he removed the rest of his clothes and then rolled her over. He lay between her legs while sucking and nibbling on her breasts, oh how he loved them and wanted to enjoy the moment.

He moved down to her stomach and flicked his tongue in and out of her navel, while both hands played with her still hard nipples. Unknowing to him, her juices were flowing freely and she was ready for him. When he moved down to her love box he finally noticed how wet her panties were, the excitement stirred even more inside of him as her covered her panties with his mouth, causing her to moan and thrust her groin into his face. He kissed the inside of her thighs before moving her panty to the side and sliding his tongue between her moist lips.

The taste of her love juices was unbelievable and he wanted more. His tongue slowly entered her hole and moved in and out of it, before he hit her clit and circled it. She was well manicured and had a strip of hair right down the center; he liked it when a woman took such detail with her body. He sucked and flicked his tongue on her clit, making her body fill with the passion she desired. You would have thought that he was at an all you can eat buffet as he worked his tongue over her mound.

Be right back he said and left the room. She removed her thong and waited for him to return. He came back with some ice cream in a bowl and a spoon; taking a small scoop from the container, he placed it on her nipples and licked it off. The cold and warm sensation sent chills throughout her body and she wanted more. Moving to her mound he placed some ice cream on her clit, and watched it as it slowly melted before he covered it with his mouth and sucked it off. This caused her to buck and moan, so he did it again, this time he didn't come up but stayed there to suck and lick her until she exploded with the most intense orgasm. Not finished yet, he causes her to have several more orgasms as he enjoyed working his tongue on her juicy fruit.

Finally she had enough and told him to stop, it was time for her to take control and she had him lie down and she began to kiss him while stroking his hard manhood. She was excited at the length of his shaft and placed her mouth on it, the feeling of her mouth on his tool made him squirm. She stopped and continued to stroke him while her mouth sucked on his nipple, making them hard and excited. The feeling was so great that he sprayed his load while she was stroking his manhood; she aimed his juice all over her chest. Thinking she would stop stroking him, he tried to pull back but she tightened her grip on his dick. He felt embarrassed by the premature ejaculation but she kept stroking him until the very last drop was expelled.

Not sure what to do to save himself from this awful moment, he just let things continue on as he wasn't sure what her thoughts were but felt he had ruined an opportunity to get with her again. Little did he know that she was not fazed by his premature ejaculation, she saw it as a compliment that he couldn't hold out but she wasn't about to let him get off so easily, especially after eating her the way he did. She was wet and needed to feel his hardness inside her, and that was she was going to do. Surely this is over he thought to himself, but she kept playing with his nipples and stoking his tool, moving her mouth between the two until he became hard again.

She gets a towel and wipes her chest off, and then she proceeds to mount him like a horse and slides his tool inside her warm slippery inviting hole. The bubbly sensation of her juices felt so good as she moved on top of him, she worked out and it showed the way she worked her muscles on top of his dick. They both began a rhythm that seemed to be choreographed. He thrust himself deep inside her as she dropped down to take every inch of him. Reaching up he squeezed her nipples and breasts while pulling down on her, every movement was met and he thrust himself even harder inside her.

The juices of her box poured down his shaft and onto his hair. Let's change position he said, sure was her reply, how do you want me? On your side he said. He slowly entered her from behind while spreading her buttock with his right hand. Using her juices, he rubbed her butt hole. He was stroking her deeply when his finger entered her butt hole, making her thrust from the excitement and achieve several more orgasms.

Finally he was ready again and pulled out to spray his load over her buttocks, taking his time to spread the juices all over her. He got a towel and cleaned her up, afterwards he took her in his arms and they just enjoyed the moment. Darn this was good they both thought, but didn't say it aloud. They both wanted more, but were content to relax for the moment. They made love again later that night, both were exhausted and lay together just looking at the ceiling, welling in their own thoughts.

He wondered if she was really ready for a committed relationship and all that he had to give to her, his mind wondered about a lot of things, especially with what he wanted to do to her sexually and what type of future they would have together, if any. Her thoughts were on the wonderful sex that she had just experienced and wondered if he was truly for real with his feelings or just saw her as another conquest for his trophy case? He didn't appear to be that way but she also wasn't sure. She had no intentions of going that far tonight but she had no regrets that she did, her thoughts were nowhere near any future plans for them, right now it was just about great sex and nothing more.

Perhaps one day he would find out what it was she really liked and what it was she wanted between the two of them, would she tell him or would he have to find out for himself? Only time would tell for the both of them. He didn't want a fuck buddy who would just call him up for a service every now and then, he wanted someone for himself but in the meantime the biggest concern on his mind was what would he do about Jasmine?

Chapter 25

Although Jasmine was upset with Le'Roi she couldn't stay mad at him, but it still bothered her that he wasn't there for her when she felt she needed someone. She had some news to share with him and he couldn't make himself available. Not that anything was wrong, but she felt that he should have been more sensitive to her feelings and to the seriousness of her message. Yes she was in another office doing work but their daily talks had become a regular routine for her, and not being able to talk to him she felt as though something was missing from her life.

It was confusing to her as she knew that she would never leave Phillip, but why was she so drawn to Le'Roi? Frustrated by this, she put the box of papers in the back of the closet and pondered her next move.

The next day she tried to call him again before she went into the office, still with no success of reaching him. That pushed her to the last straw as she felt that she had to go to Columbia as soon as she could to see what was going on. While she hadn't finished the auditing of the transactions, her mindset was on Le'Roi and what he was doing and what was so important that he couldn't answer her calls and talk with her.

When she was walking down the hall to her office she saw Tom looking as if he had just come out of her office, but why was he in there she asked herself? Not wanting to say anything, she went in and closed the door behind her, and instinctively went to the desk to see if the recorder was still there. She could tell it had been moved and now at least she may have found out who put it there, but why was still the question. Jasmine asked for a personal day to take care of some business, yes, she was going to Columbia to see Le'Roi and then be back in Atlanta before the day was over.

Le'Roi left Colleen's place later that evening the day before after showering; when he got in his car he realized that he had several calls from Jasmine. She left a message on the first one but none on the other calls; he figured he would call her back in the morning.

As he woke up that morning, he started having mixed feelings about what just happened last night at Colleen's place. Strangely, he was beginning to feel guilt over being with her, as if he had just cheated on Jasmine, he didn't understand why the hell he felt that way but he didn't like it. His mind went to the numerous times that Jasmine called him and under normal circumstances he would have called her right back, that's if he had missed the call. Now he found himself avoiding her calls as he was being drawn to Colleen.

He knew that he had to break it off with Jasmine if he was ever going to have a normal relationship, but how would he do it was the question. Jasmine was very vulnerable and needing someone to make her feel special at this point in her life, Le'Roi understood that and also recognized that he enjoyed talking to her, but he just couldn't get past Phillip.

He got out of bed and begins preparing himself for the workday. He had his usual routine of coffee and breakfast, it might have been better that he ate out that morning but he saw no reason to change what he had been doing before. He was about to leave for work when his cell phone rang, he saw it was Jasmine and decided to answer it. Hello, he said.

Hi, where were you last night Jasmine asked?

I was just out.

Then why didn't you answer you cell phone? I have called you several times and you didn't even bother to call me back.

I left it in the car.

Why did you do that she asked? Did you go out and get it this morning? I want to know what is really going on as you have become a bit distant lately.

I just didn't want to take it with me, he said, wondering why the line of questioning as she sounded very suspicious. Look, I am about to walk out the door and head to the office, I'll hit you back up when I get in the car.

Okay she said.

When he opened the front door to leave he was totally surprised to see Jasmine outside of it, he quickly pulled her inside and scanned the street before closing the door.

What are you doing here he asked?

I wanted to know if you were here alone.

Of course I am, why the hell wouldn't I be he replied sternly.

Look, I am not trying to run your life but when you didn't answer my calls and then I couldn't reach you I just became a bit worried.

Worried about what, he asked? Whether or not I am out seeing someone else? That's what it sounds like with all of the questions. You took a very big chance coming over here, what if you were followed?

Why are you getting so defensive, is there someone or something I need to know about? Besides, you worry too much Le'Roi; Phillip doesn't care about me or anything that I do, now damn it trust me on this. Now answer this for me, why would I think you were out seeing someone else?

Le'Roi felt this was his best time to tell her about the other woman, that he was having feelings for someone else, but he wasn't sure if they even had any prospects for a relationship and decided to keep those thoughts to himself, but he was also tired of sneaking around to see Jasmine and even so was more worried about her husband and what he would do if he found out about their relationship.

Let's talk later as I am about to be late for work, Le'Roi said.

That's fine, I am going back to Atlanta anyway but Le'Roi, I'm not finished with this conversation. In fact why don't you come down for the weekend, I need some attention and you have been neglecting me.

I can't make any promises, but I will tell you that I don't like the insinuation that you are making.

Man you really are sensitive, if I thought something was really going on I would have said so.

Meanwhile Tom called Phillip's office on the premise of discussing some proposed planning. You know I don't like talking about business here, in fact let me call you when I get outside Phillip said. Better yet, you also get in your car and you go for a ride and then call me when you get someplace private.

Tom called Phillip back about twenty minutes later, now what is so damn important that you had to talk about right now Phillip asked?

I think we may have a problem, I'm not sure of this but I don't think we can trust James.

You better have a damn good reason for this as you are really wasting my time, I don't work on thoughts, I work with facts Phillip said.

Well you know we put the recorder in her office like you instructed.

Yes, and???

For some reason James kept going back down there. He said he was going for walks and I followed him a couple of times and each time I saw him enter her office, but I don't know what he was doing there. I thought I saw him change the tape one time but we always do that together to cover our backs.

Was she in the office when he was there?

No.

Phillip wondered what this meant with James and why he was in and out of Jasmine's office so much. He had to find out what the hell was going on and quickly. Don't talk to James about this but keep and eye on him and her, if you ever see them meet anywhere or get wind of a meeting between the two of them, you call me right away.

Okay Tom said.

They departed and went back to their respective locations; James met Tom when he arrived back at the office.

Hey man what's up James asked?

Nothing much.

Late today huh?

Naw man, I just had to make a quick run, that's all.

Is everything okay?

Yeah, everything is fine. Let me get to work before I fall behind Tom said.

James had the sneaky suspicion that there was more to the conversation than Tom was willing to let on. Once they were tight together but lately they just seem to be distant associates, his display of actions today said that perhaps something was wrong, maybe he needed to watch him.

Le'Roi's drive to the office was a difficult one due to the emotions he was experiencing, as he wanted to tell Jasmine about Colleen but he also didn't like her questioning his whereabouts. He wanted to break it off with Jasmine and fully pursue Colleen, but not being sure what his prospects were he didn't want to just shut off everything. Damn this made him seem like a player, keeping something on the side until he could get something else. But the one on the side didn't belong to him so why did he feel somewhat of a commitment to her? Besides, she was becoming demanding and he didn't like that.

When he arrived at his office there was a message on the door from the vice president asking him to come see him as soon as possible. He sat his things down and went to the V.P.'s office. He was being sent to an office in Maryland as a consultant and was expected to be gone for about two weeks. Later that night he went to see Colleen and told her about the trip, he stayed awhile and they shared some intimate moments but nothing that had progressed to the point that it did last night. That didn't bother Le'Roi because he needed to figure some things out in his mind anyway.

He also called Jasmine and told her about the trip which meant that the weekend that she thought was going to happen would have to wait until a later time. Of course she became upset about him not being able to spend time with her that weekend, that solidified his thinking about her becoming demanding and having expectations of him.

Chapter 26

With Le'Roi away in Maryland for the next couple of weeks, Jasmine took that time to complete her transaction review of the documents that she had to look at, her office conversations were strictly business as she knew the recorder was under the desk. It was only when she got home that she would go through the papers in the box that was originally placed outside her office door. There were procedures in place to validate and verify all transactions that occurs, in this case it seems that all of them were bypassed, which means that there had to be at least two people involved in executing the Zylander transactions she reasoned.

Every day she checked to see if the recorder placed under the desk had been moved, once she opened it up and put a mark in the corner of the tape, she was surprised to see that it had been replaced the next day when she came to work. She still had no clue as to who it was that wanted to record her conversations, and more importantly, why?

Phillip on the other hand was still being his typical self, except he was beginning to feel that his world was starting to crumble. His business associates didn't like the way things were going and he saw how they dealt with things that appeared to be loose ends. Add to that the fact that there was distrust among the group between Tom and James. Maybe it was time to get out of the business and walk away, but would his business associates allow that and at what cost to him?

He had to find out what James was up to and if Tom was credible in what he was saying, it appeared that he couldn't trust anyone and if one person spoke it could take them all down. Still in the back of his mind was his business associates and how they seem to know what was going on in his world. Yes, he needed to head off any potential problems before something drastic happened, he didn't care about the guys in the circle but he didn't want Jasmine mixed up in anything, because knowing the type of person she was she wouldn't be involved with his scheme and would also most likely be the person most likely to tell what was going on.

Phillip knew he had to take a trip to Atlanta just for a day or two to settle some things and see what was really going on. He arrived there two days later and Jasmine was totally shocked to see him when he entered her office, hey babe he said. He then walks over and gives her a hug that she hadn't had from him in a long time, one that was filled with warmth and passion, followed by a kiss.

Phillip, why didn't you tell me you were coming? Is anything wrong she asked?

No baby, I just needed a break and to tie some loose ends up here, that's all.

Okay, it is so good to see you. Have you been home yet?

No, I drove straight here this morning. Let me get going so that I can do what I need to do and we can go out for dinner tonight.

That sounds good.

Cool, you pick the place he said.

Phillip heads off and Jasmine wonders why he is being so nice to her. This was way out of character for him and was a cause of concern for her. She figured in due time the answer would be revealed.

Phillip heads straight to the office where Tom and James each worked and told them to meet him for lunch. Both men were shocked to even see that Phillip was in town, Tom was supposed to watch James for Phillip and now he was wondering what Phillip found out and more importantly why didn't he tell him that he was coming to Atlanta?

They meet for lunch and Phillip looks both men in the eye and ask if there is anything they need to tell him? They looked at each other and said no, then look back at Phillip.

Then tell me James, what is it that keeps you going to Jasmine's office repeatedly Phillip replies.

What are you talking about?

I know that you have been going down to Jasmine's office and I want to know why?

James looks at Tom, who stares straight ahead. So this is what's been going on James says. I asked you Tom what was going on and you said nothing, and now I am being questioned about why I went into Jasmine's office?

James, you never answered the question so I am going to ask you one more time, what were you doing in Jasmine's office?

I went down there to check the recorder, that's the truth.

Don't you and Tom usually do that together?

Yes, but I have a suspicion that she knows the tape recorder is there and I have been checking on it.

What makes you think she knows about it?

One day I was walking by and my mind told me to check it, since she wasn't in I did. When I looked under the desk I could see that the recorder had been moved, so I rewound the tape and listened to it. You could tell she knew something was up because her whole demeanor changed, and you could hear it in her voice. Besides, the tape wasn't completely at the point where it shut off.

Why didn't you tell me about this before now, Phillip asks?

I needed proof, I couldn't just come to you and accuse your wife of something if I didn't have my shit together, you would have kicked my ass.

What about the time I saw you remove a tape Tom yells.

I changed the tape because I didn't want her to erase what we already had before her demeanor changed; the tape is in the safe place along with the rest of them that we have collected. If your dumb ass had been paying attention about what we are supposed to be doing instead of trying to keep tabs on me you would have known that.

Tom was mad and about to say something when Phillip cut him off and said if that is true then we don't have a problem, at least not among ourselves. However, if it turns out to be false then there will be consequences to pay. Tom was again about to say something when Phillip raised his hand to cut him off the second time.

James looks at Tom with a stern look and says, you are the cause of all this and if you had just come to me I would have explained everything, but instead your bitch ass runs to Phillip as if I did something wrong. Don't ever say a motherfucking word to me again, he says.

Knock this shit off, what is done is done, and I just hope for your sake the tape is there.

Oh it's in there; you can guarantee that James replied.

Then let's go and see Phillip said as he raised himself from the table. They headed back to the office and meet at the location holding the tapes, each man arrives separately but none enters the room until all are present. Just as James had said the tape was there, Phillip played the tape that James told him about and sure enough the manner in which Jasmine handled herself gave a sense of knowing that she knew the recorder was there. He also hears her talking to someone about Zylander but there is no way to tell whom since she was on the phone. I want it removed and put away Phillip orders, when, asked James? Today damn it, do it today when she leaves.

Phillip heads straight to Jasmine's office and says, hey babe, let's get out of here a bit early today, it's been awhile since we spent some quality time together. Jasmine had a shocked look on her face, as this was not the same man that she had been living with for the past few years. They both leave the office and arrive at home in their individual cars, each shower and then head out for a quiet evening starting with dinner.

When Tom saw that Phillip and Jasmine departed the building, he went and took the tape recorder from under her desk. As he was leaving the office he noticed the executive director watching him, though he didn't say anything to him, his look became a major concern for Tom.

When Tom arrived back at the office, he immediately went to James to give him the recorder; James refused to take it since he felt betrayed by Tom's actions and simply walked away, leaving Tom standing there by himself. Tom looked around and saw that the executive director had followed him into the office and now he felt trapped. Tom, in my office the executive director said, and bring that with you as he pointed to the device Tom was holding. Tom's heart began racing one hundred miles an hour, what would he do, if Phillip found out there would be hell to pay. Tom followed the executive director to his office and closed the door when they entered the room.

Phillip and Jasmine had a very nice evening with dinner followed by a visit to a local jazz club, Phillip made sure that no one would interrupt them so they both left their cell phones at home, and they even turned them off. The atmosphere was very mellow as usually it was the older crowd that frequented the establishment, there were some people there that knew Phillip and they all seem to go out of their way to speak to him. The evening was very nice but Jasmine couldn't fully enjoy it as her mind was centered on Phillip and the way he was acting. She said acting because this was way out of his norm, which kept her wondering what he was up to.

They left the club and went home when Phillip takes her into his arms and kisses her passionately, their lips hungrily seeking the others. While in the bed he caresses her body before they make love. While she loves Phillip this seems strange to her, her mind moves back and forth from Le'Roi to Phillip and what he is doing. She wasn't trying to make a comparison between the two but Phillip just seems out of place to her. He goes down on her and gives her the pleasure that she loves to receive, when he finishes she moves to give him the same when he stops her and says "this isn't about me, it's all about you tonight". The words were comforting to her ears as she lay back and felt Phillip enter her wet love box; they make love until he is exhausted and lies beside her.

Gently he takes her into his arms as they lay together. While the feeling is good, Jasmine is cautious, this is not her husband. The earlier man that she knew would have done these things but the one she has known for the last few years was not the same man. Then there was the other part, things were so strange to her that even his touched seemed to be scripted; the intimate lovemaking scene was purely more mechanical than emotional.

Perhaps she had become so accustomed to being with Le'Roi and the way he moved his hands on her body, maybe this is why Phillip's touch felt out of place to her. She was thinking too much and realized it when Phillip interrupted her thoughts and says to her, if there was something that I needed to know you would tell me, right? Yes I would she replies, knowing that there was some things she surely couldn't tell him. The room was very quiet as if Phillip was waiting for her to fill in the blanks. So in saying that is there something that you want to tell me he said? Her mind is going crazy as she believes he had found out about her and Le'Roi, she hesitates and then finally says no, now what would I possibly have to tell you?

Nothing, I was just wondering if you would, that's all. Phillip could sense the uneasiness in Jasmine's words, he wanted to be rough with her but felt that any attempt to manhandle her may cause her to do something with the information. While he was laying there trying to play his wife for information, he didn't realize that he would have bigger concerns.

Jasmine suspected that there was more to Phillip than what he told her and now she knew that he was looking for something, she wasn't sure if he knew about Le'Roi but she also knew that she had to break things off with him. The one piece to the puzzle that troubled her was the fact that she was in Atlanta, Phillip in Columbia, and Le'Roi was now in Maryland for a couple of weeks, so how could he have ever tied the two of them together?

If he did suspect something he would have to be the one to present the evidence to her as she was not going to tell him anything, at this point.

Chapter 27

Tom's visit to the executive director's office was not a pleasant one, he was caught coming out of Jasmine's office with the voice recorder and kept asking what he was using it for and more importantly what was on it? Tom didn't want to answer any questions and intentionally stalled him out, which frustrated the executive director so much that he called security to make sure Tom didn't leave the room or the building.

About an hour later two men show up and enter the office, they identify themselves as F.B.I. agents. Tom didn't know it but he had just committed a federal crime by recording a conversation of someone without their permission. He was read his rights, the voice recorder was confiscated as evidence, and he was taken to a federal facility and booked. The executive director was concerned about what was on the tape as it may have contained privileged company information. He wanted to listen to it but because it was evidence he was denied the opportunity.

When James heard about Tom being called to the executive director's office he became a little concerned, he did not know that the executive director had seen Tom with the recording device, so he dismissed it as normal company business. It was later that he found out that Tom was escorted out of the building by two men and placed in a black sedan, no one knew why he was with the men but plenty of speculation flew around the office. James knew that he had to tell Phillip, as he was the one guy that could find out what was going on, he tried calling his cell phone and kept getting his voice mail. He was not going to leave a message as that was against the rules, voice contact only, no messages.

Tom was given a lawyer while he was at the federal holding station; he had not talked to the investigators and would only do so with his lawyer, the executive director was also at the station as he had to fill out a report since he called the federal agents. While he was there he was still hoping to get to listen to the tape or at least get a copy of it, the answer was still no. The federal agents tried to pry information out of Tom by using threats and intimidation acts, they were humorous to Tom as there was nothing that they could say or do to him to force him to talk. When his lawyer arrived the federal agents got down to serious business, Tom was looking at about five years of jail time for the recording, and if it proved to have sensitive company information on it, the years would begin to accumulate.

Tom knew that there were no company secrets on the recording, but with Jasmine's conversations being on it he knew that anyone that listened to the tape would only open the door for more questions. Shit he thought, how the hell could I let this happen? What if they found out about the other tapes and what they were doing with the Zylander Company? He reasoned that they all would get life in prison and he was not about to go to jail for something that he didn't even come up with, he was just a participant.

Then again, they treat all participants the same as the mastermind behind the scheme. He needed to work a deal with them but he also needed protection, for surely Phillip would come after him to keep him quiet. Okay he said, what if I were to give you some information that would prove that a crime was committed? Depends on what it is one agent said. No, I want to speak to the executive director along with my lawyer before I say anymore.

They brought the executive director in and the three of them sat down and talked about what information Tom had and what he wanted in exchange for it, Tom would only say that Phillip was the key to everything and wouldn't say anything else unless he was allowed to go home that night to retrieve his information, and be provided protection after he gave his details tomorrow. Reluctantly the executive director agreed to Tom's conditions because he wanted to know more, and he figured he could wait until morning to figure out what was going on, and what Phillip had to do with anything. If Tom failed to provide the information that he promised, the deal was off and he would be pursued for the maximum sentence in jail.

The fed's released Tom on the condition that he would be there tomorrow with the information that he promised or the deal was off. An agent would take him to get his car from the company parking lot and then follow him home. When Tom arrived at his place the front door was ajar, he turned and looked at the agent who got out of the car and followed him to the door. As Tom when in he turned on the lights and saw that his place had been ransacked, they checked the house and found that no one was there, suddenly Tom thought about the information and went to the freezer and saw that the papers he had stashed there were gone.

NO he screamed! What's wrong the agent asked? I am screwed he said, the information that I was going to present tomorrow was here in the freezer and now it is gone; we have to call this in. That won't be necessary, the agent said. Stunned, Tom turned around and asked why not? Because you have become a liability that we can no longer afford, at the point Tom saw the agent pull his hand from behind his back and suddenly the room went dark.

The next day comes very quickly for Phillip, he had fun with Jasmine but he didn't find out what he needed to know. He had done everything that he thought would make her tell him what she knew but it was to no avail, it didn't matter to him, as he was willing to do whatever it took to get what he wanted in the end. She didn't have to know that he wasn't sincere and the truth being told, he couldn't wait to shower that morning and wash her off of him.

After showering and getting dressed he noticed that she was still lying in bed, he turned his cell phone on and saw that he had five missed calls from James. He called him and James told him about the situation with Tom being taken to the executive director's office and then being escorted from the building by two men.

Shit man, why the hell didn't you tell me this last night?

You said no messages, so I was sticking to the rules. Phillip raising his voice caught Jasmine's attention, realizing this Phillip hangs up and heads straight out the door for the office, he didn't even bother to say goodbye to Jasmine. After he leaves she contemplates calling Le'Roi and telling him about Phillips behavior and questions, she thinks they should cool it for a while but for some reason she doesn't call him. The best thing to do she decided was to go into the office and let the President know that she has finished the review.

When Phillip arrived at the office he notices that there is a strange and somber mood about the building, he finds out that Tom was killed last night during a home burglary. Apparently someone broke into his home and he confronted the intruder and somehow during the struggle Tom was shot in the head and killed instantly, the house was in complete shambles and there were no shell casings found during a search of the house. Right now the police have no suspects identified with the robbery and killing, or any leads.

Phillip walks over to James and nods his head, indicating they need to talk. As he turned to leave the executive director takes him by the arm and tells him to come to his office, when Phillip walks into the room he sees one of the company lawyers present. The executive director informs Phillip that he has been placed on administrative leave pending the outcome of an internal investigation into the allegations that Tom made prior to his death.

Phillip is escorted to his office to retrieve some personal belongings and is surprised to find that someone has already been through the things in his office. Not wanting to arouse any suspicion, he keeps quiet and takes his few items and leaves the building. Later he calls

James and Coleman to have them meet him at their usual spot in the mall parking lot at ten o'clock that night. He then heads to the bank to check his account and is surprised to see that the money he was paying for the rent of that stupid bitch hasn't been taken out for last month, hell he had forgotten about her anyway.

He takes all of his money out of his local account then heads to the restaurant to see the woman whose rent he had been paying. He finds out that she stopped working there about one month ago and no one knows where she went. Damn it he thought, right now he really needed someone to talk to and he couldn't find anyone. Of course he still has no remorse over the way he has treated any of the people he has come across during his lifetime, and only focuses on his selfish motives.

He calls Coleman but no one answers his phone either, man what the hell is going on he asks himself. That's it, he knows why all of this is happening, Jasmine has found out the truth and she has shared it with others, which is the reason for the internal investigation. The only question that remains in his mind is how did she put the pieces together once she found out? He had been very careful to cover his tracks but apparently he wasn't good enough, or maybe she was just that smart? Either way he would have to find out and wouldn't rest until he confronted her with this, but not now. Let's see where this investigation is headed, I wouldn't want to give them any ammunition to use against me just in case they don't have all the facts he thought to himself. Yes, for now he would play it cool and sit back and wait, then that would determine his course of action.

While all of this is going on Le'Roi still maintains his communications with Colleen, so much to the point that while he thinks about Jasmine she is no longer the center of attention for him. He doesn't know when the thoughts of her begin to decline, but rationalizes it to the time when she showed up at his house unexpectedly. Meanwhile Colleen decides that she wants to come to Maryland to see Le'Roi, which he doesn't mind at all. He hasn't called Jasmine in a few days and she hasn't called him, which was even better. Le'Roi figures he and Colleen would have a small cookout at the park and take things from there. Colleen was so excited about the prospect that she agreed to come sooner rather than later.

When he arrived at the office Le'Roi checked his calendar and made sure that no appointments or meetings were scheduled for Friday afternoon. Now he had to only focus on what he was planning for him and Colleen's next get together. Le'Roi remembered how Colleen spoke about being pampered, so his idea on this was to line the room with candles and spread rose petals of different colors around the place. He would bring a couple of movies, one adult and one regular movie just so that they could have something to do in between their lovemaking sessions. He would bring a cooler with drinks on ice and something relaxing to wear.

Later that week Le'Roi had everything worked out and planned within his mind, he and Colleen would go to the next town over and have a small picnic in the park. He would bring along a small grill or find a park that had the grills already, some meat and two side dishes along with the appropriate cutlery items. The local market makes this very easy as he doesn't have to prepare anything, hell even the meat would be pre-seasoned. That would be the ultimate and it would give the appearance that he had prepared everything himself, even though he had a little help it didn't hurt anything, for Colleen would never know the difference.

After that they would stop off at a restaurant and have a couple of drinks before heading to his hotel room. There he would have the perfect setup for her and she didn't have a clue as to what would happen. Colleen was a sight to behold and the best part about her was the fact that she never questioned him about what he did or whom he was doing it with. She never asked him about his work or even questioned him about what he did during his off time; this made her really special to him for she liked Le'Roi very much and felt that they had something special, of course this made him feel the same way.

The only drawback he had about the relationship was the fact that he always had to call her, and she would only call him to return his call. Overall though, he liked the prospect of a serious committed relationship with a woman that he could call his own and not have to share. As strange as it may seem, he was still having feelings for Jasmine and the only way for him to let those feelings subside was to find a way to get rid of Jasmine, but the strange thing was he had no commitment to her as she was married and he was not. Why was the attraction to her so strong? He didn't know why, he just knew it was there.

Colleen came to Maryland Thursday night; they went to dinner and back to his hotel room. Le'Roi had planned to be the perfect gentlemen that night, besides he wanted to test a theory of his and see if she would make any initial movement towards him if he did not initiate the intimacy between them. After they sat and talked for a while he took a shower and came out to find her in bed, the look of the outline of her body under the covers was making him aroused, but he kept to his word and didn't initiate anything. He got in bed and curled up under her and noticed that she was wearing panties and a tee shirt; to make sure he kept things into perspective he placed his manhood between his legs and waited for her actions.

When he awoke the next morning he noticed that she was grinding against his body, his manhood was no longer tucked away between his legs, but was at a full erection as he wanted to get inside of her. Reaching over he squeezes her breasts while playing with a nipple, her breathing starts to quicken and he can tell that she is ready for him. She moves her body faster against his when she stops and removes her clothes, he gets a condom from the drawer and puts it on. Colleen climbs on top of him and kisses his chest, flicking her tongue at his nipples while inserting his hard dick inside her juicy box. Her body bounces on top of him as she is already working on a climax, he places his hands on her hips and helps her go deeper down on his tool. Any thoughts of analyzing his theory would have to wait until later.

He moves his hands down to her buttocks and grabs each cheek to pull them apart so that every inch of him can be inside her, she moans even more and then she stops moving and begins shaking. He stops his movements and just pushes himself deeper into that body of hers, when she finishes he turns her over on her stomach and strokes her from behind. She is into the rhythm now as each time he pulls back to go deeper her legs raises and presses against his to push him deeper inside her, while she simultaneously raises her hips for his penetration. He does this until he reaches his own point and lays on top of her while she contracts her muscles to milk every drop of his cum out of his dick and into her. This was definitely a good way to wake up in the morning, and he hoped the rest of the day would be just as good.

Although the day was cloudy and there was a slight chance of rain, Le'Roi was determined to make sure that his plans would still be carried out. After a light breakfast he and Colleen walked about town for a bit doing nothing particular, just spending some time together. When the lunchtime came around, Colleen wanted to stop and get something to eat but Le'Roi has already taken care of that. While she was showering he took that opportunity to pack everything into the car trunk so that she wouldn't be suspicious. They rode together to the next town, she was surprised when they stopped at a park saying, "I thought we were going to get some lunch"? We are he replied, right here. Colleen didn't know what was going on but Le'Roi assured her to just play along. He took the items out of the trunk of the car, the grill, cooler, and two blankets.

He set the grill up and started the fire; he had already prepped the grill with the charcoal which made things a bit easier. Then he spread the blankets out on the lawn so Colleen could relax, of course her mind was in awe as she never expected anything like this. Yes he generally thought things through and this was no exception. The aroma of burning charcoal filled the air and tickled Colleen's senses, when the coals were ready Le'Roi opened the cooler and placed some chicken and steak on the grill. Her mouth begins to water from the smell of the meat being seared by the heat, as it was just overwhelming. She was really hungry from their lovemaking routine this morning and the walking around, so she couldn't wait to sink her teeth into something good.

Realizing he forgot the plates and cutlery; he walks back to the car and retrieves the other bag. He walks back to the blankets and carefully sets a place out for the two of them, he realizes that his inattention to the grill has caused the fire to rise and the meat could begin to burn; he rushes over and sees that one steak is just beginning to be burned but the chicken is fine. Hey he thought, nothing wrong with burnt offerings, this caused him to laugh internally as the first time he heard that was from a preacher talking about how his wife couldn't cook.

Le'Roi set the side dishes out and served the meat, the meal was rather delicious and Colleen was totally surprised at how well he thought about this and put things together. This is the quality that she admired most about Le'Roi, his uncanny ability to think things out through the smallest detail. While there were many other things she liked and admired about him, he still never ceased to amaze her with the things that he did. After finishing lunch, Le'Roi packed things up and they stopped at a local place and had some drinks.

When they arrived later at the motel, Le'Roi told her to wait outside until he told her to come in. He summoned her in and she saw that he had lit candles throughout the room and she heard water running in the bathroom. Le'Roi told her to relax and prepare for her bath, while she gets undressed he goes and turns off the water and closes the door behind him. He appears a few moments later wearing some shorts and a tank top, and places his clothes on the dresser. She walks into the bathroom and enters the tub and simply relaxes under the feel of warm water and bubbles. After she completes her bath she enters the room and finds that he has spread rose petals of all colors on the bed. Lie down he says, and she promptly obeys.

The feel of the rose petals beneath her body is strange; they are cold and somewhat prickly. He stands over her and takes off his tank top shirt, grabs a bottle of warming oil from the night stand and pours it on her chest; he kneels down over her and rubs the oil on her body. It feels a bit chilly at first but as the oil warms up the sensation feels good to her.

Le'Roi moves down to her legs and her feet before having her roll over. He picks the rose petals off her back and tosses them on the floor, before getting off her and removing his shorts. Colleen realizes this and assumes that he is totally naked along with her; his throbbing dick confirmed her suspicions. Le'Roi rubs her shoulders, her back, buttocks, thighs, and her calves. His hands feel good on her body as she totally relaxes and enjoys the moment. Le'Roi gets off the bed and grabs a towel, he wipes the oil off the backside of her body, she tries to roll over but her stops her, not yet he said.

Chapter 28

Jasmine meanwhile has gone through all of the paperwork that mysteriously appeared at her office, she didn't know who put it there or even who was connected with it, all she really had were some paper transactions that were not in the system database. Yes Phillip was very interested in the Zylander Company but what was his tie to the company? She had finished the review of all the transactions that Phillip had suggested to the President, and she found nothing out of the ordinary, everything was in place.

She was about to make an appointment to see the President when the phone rings and the executive director's secretary asks her to come to his office, she immediately hangs up and goes to see him. Please come in and sit down he says to her, Jasmine sits and waits for him to explain why he wanted to see her. She notices that there are two gentlemen in the room, one she recognizes as one of the firm's lawyers and the other she has never met before. Since no one bothered to provide introductions she was a bit bothered by it and wondered what was going on.

Is there anything going on that you want to let me know about, he asked.

What do you mean sir?

Jasmine, Phillip has been suspended pending the outcome of an internal investigation based on information received from someone else.

What information, and from whom she asked?

That's not important right now the other gentleman said.

I can handle this; the executive director said, but what we want to know is what information can you shed on this.

I have no idea what you are talking about sir Jasmine said as she was starting to become very irritated. What is all this about?

Not wanting to tip his hand, the executive director told her this, I have spoken with the President and we all feel it is your best interest that you cease work on the transaction reviews and go back to Columbia to help with the reorganization.

I have finished the transaction review and was about to inform the President when I got the call to come to your office.

Did you find anything out of the ordinary?

No sir I didn't she responded.

Very well then, I expect that you will report back to Columbia in the morning. This gentleman will escort you to your office and then to your car.

Is that really necessary she asked?

It's the best thing to do at this point and Jasmine; until this matter is cleared up you will not be allowed back into your office without an escort. By the way, what was Phillip's relationship with Tom?

I don't know, why do you ask?

Tom was found dead in his home; apparently he was killed by an intruder.

Oh my God she gasped.

Tom was supposed to provide some information and details that dealt with him and Phillip, did you know that?

Sir I really have no idea as to what you are talking about, what type of information?

That's all for now, officer will you escort Jasmine to her office and then to her car?

Jasmine gets up and walks out, with the other guy right behind her. She goes into her office and grabs her things; she wanted to look under the desk to see if the recorder was still there and if it had anything to do with the investigation. She picks her keys up off the desk and drops them to the floor, which was her excuse to see if the recorder was still there and when she looked it was gone. She picks the keys up and moves towards the door, the gentlemen or officer as he was referred to, follows behind and he walks her to the parking lot, he stands there until she drives away, then he goes back to the executive director's office.

Jasmine wondered about the line of questioning and what the connection was between Tom and her husband, she picks up her phone and tries to call Phillip, she wants to know what the hell is going on and why is he being investigated. He doesn't answer his phone so she heads straight for the house, when she arrives he isn't there either. First she was concerned that he may have known about her affair with Le'Roi and now she realizes that he may have been talking about something totally different, this crap was really starting to get out of hand to her. Maybe Phillip knew what was going on and was fishing for information from her, which would explain why he was so nice and cordial to her but kept asking if she had anything to tell him. She was going to call Le'Roi later, maybe he knew what was happening.

Phillip was still driving around town trying to collect his thoughts when he figured that he'd meet the remaining members together and discuss strategy in the event this was about their dealings. James answered when he was called and agreed to meet at the usual place, but Coleman still had not answered his phone nor had he called Phillip back. Man this shit is crazy, where the fuck is he Phillip thought to himself.

He saw where Jasmine called him but she wasn't his primary concern right now, she probably just wants another fuck he thought. That bitch can wait. Phillip went to a bar and sat down for a drink and collects his thoughts, how the hell can everything that was going so good get so fucked up so quickly? He didn't have the answer but he knew that he had to put a wrap on things or his business associates may be paying him a visit.

While at the bar he was looking at the television but not really paying attention to it when the local station broke in with a special report, apparently the body of a male had been found in a wooden area with his throat slashed. That really didn't concern Phillip as things like this was happening all the time. The reporter described the body and still Phillip didn't give a crap about it until she identified the man as being Coleman Young. Phillip sat straight up and stared directly at the television, his mouth was wide open. His mind begin to try and comprehend what was happening, first Tom and now Coleman. This could be a coincidence but what are the odds? Phillip was not in a gambling mood so he picked up his phone and called James to tell him the meeting was off, but James didn't answer his phone.

Damn it, I have to let him know the meeting is off. Phillip leaves the bar and begins driving to James's house, this was definitely out of the norm but this was an exception. As Phillip was driving he sensed that he was being followed, he made a couple of turns to see if the car behind him was still there, it was. Now came the change of plan, he very well couldn't go to James's house so he decided to continue driving and then figure out what to do. After a while the car left but it seemed that a different one was following him, he decided to turn into a gas station and see what was going on. He reached for the gun that he kept in the car just in case something like this ever happened. He didn't know what was about to happen, but he wanted to be ready just in case.

Back in Maryland, the sound of music fills the room but it isn't the normal slow music that Colleen has become accustomed to with Le'Roi, she turns over and sees that he is wearing a black g-string bikini. What are you wearing she asks? Just sit back and enjoy the show he said, as he moves his hips in a gyrating fashion that causes her to laugh out loud; he continues his dance, not caring what it seemed like to her. Colleen comments out loud, "man you really don't have any rhythm", where were you when it was handed out? Le'Roi completes his dance with a booty shake rendition at the end of the song, and then slowly creeps up to the bed where Colleen lay.

He kisses her on the lips, neck, and breasts, taking time to savor every spot. He slides his way down to her groin area and feverishly attacks her love box, he feels her wetness as he rubs his lips over her clit and the outside of her lips. She begins to moan and wiggle beneath him, her breathing picks up and she gets into the moment. She says out loud "oh Tony this feels so good". Le'Roi stops and looks at her with searing eyes, what's wrong she asks? Le'Roi looks at her and wanted to ask who the hell Tony was? But rather than get into a heated debate he continued on with what he was doing.

They continue on with their lovemaking until both have climaxed a couple of times. Colleen could sense that something was wrong, as Le'Roi seemed different than what he was earlier. She wanted to know what was going on with him but each time she asked he always replied with "nothing is wrong". Colleen was no fool and she knew that something was going on, but how would she find out if he was not willing to tell her?

Later that evening Le'Roi looked at Colleen and asked, who is Tony? How do you know Tony she replied? Because that was the name that you called me while I was eating you, so who is this guy? Trying not to look shocked, she quickly tried to compose her thoughts. I was going to tell you Le'Roi that I am seeing someone else; I really hadn't planned to do all of this with you as I wanted to be upfront and honest with you about what was going on.

So why did you come here he asked?

I just wanted to see you again and I also felt that you had a right to know about my new friend face to face.

So is that all I was to you, just a friend?

Well, yeah. I mean what else did you think was happening between us?

Colleen, I thought that we made a connection of some sort; I was really ready to settle down with you.

When did I ever give you the impression that I wanted to settle down with you? I mean we had some good times but you are not the type of man I want to settle down with?

Le'Roi felt his heart had hit the floor, why, what's wrong with me?

Le'Roi you are married to your job and besides, I don't know who it is you are seeing but I don't have your undivided attention. I saw that from day one, while I am not always with you it seems that your mind is off on someone or somewhere else.

Well if you felt that way why didn't you say something to me?

Like what? That I know or think that you are with someone else? Come on man; think about what you are saying. Look, we had some good times and let's just leave it at that.

Le'Roi never thought or felt about Colleen the same way after that, his feelings toward her had definitely changed, as he felt a bit of betrayal. He was hurt as he felt that she only saw him as a piece of meat and nothing meaningful. Here he was with two women in his life and neither one belonged to him, one didn't want to be with him and the other he couldn't be with. After a discussion they decided that she would leave in the morning, and as their time went on they never got to watch the movie they had intended, that night the tension was still felt as they didn't cuddle as they did the night before.

Le'Roi now felt that he understood why she never made the first move towards intimacy with him, as she was wrestling with the point of being with Tony as he was with Jasmine. In a lot of ways they were alike and their situations seem to parallel each other, he couldn't be mad with her for what she was feeling as he was the one that assumed they could have a life together. Then again, he still had Jasmine somewhere in his mind.

Jasmine called Le'Roi but he didn't answer his phone and this time she did leave a message asking him to call her immediately. She had so much to talk to him about but she just couldn't reach him, this was causing her issues within herself because he had always been there for her and now he seemed so distant from her. Even the time she showed up at his house fully expecting to find someone there but didn't, maybe it was her own mind playing tricks on her and perhaps she was expecting too much of him.

With his trip to Maryland about to wrap up, she couldn't wait for him to get back so that they could reconnect. While this was what she wanted she also knew that she had to end it with Le'Roi, as Phillip was getting too close to the situation for her and the comfort level was not what it was before. She figured they would have one last encounter before she told him that they had to stop, yes, one more encounter. In the morning she would head back to Columbia to finish up the reorganization plan or hand it off to someone else and then come back to Atlanta to be with Phillip, regardless of his past indiscretions, she was going to be the perfect wife for him in his time of need.

Phillip's stop at the gas station proved useful, as the cars he thought were following him were no where in sight, he could go home but what was the point? Jasmine was probably there and by now surely she had heard of the suspension and would have a thousand questions, he wasn't in the mood for that shit right now so he figured that after meeting James he would go to a motel and spend the night there, then go home and face Jasmine. All he knew was that she had done him in and he would go home and deal with her, yes, that bitch was gone and would be left with nothing. Even the house that her mother slept in would be gone and then what would she do? Hell that wasn't his problem and he was determined to show her just how badly she fucked herself. He again tried to call James and still couldn't get a hold of him, later that night he went to the rendezvous point anyway, but James wasn't there.

Phillip waited for about thirty minutes when he decided he had enough, as he was about to leave a group of cars swarmed around him and blocked his car in place, some guys got out with guns drawn and yelled "federal agents, turn off the car". Phillip hesitated and thought about grabbing his own gun, but clearly he was outnumbered and they had the advantage. Reason and common sense came into play and before he did anything else, his mind saw his world crumbling down and his thoughts reflected back to Jasmine and how could she do him like this when he has done so much for her.

Phillip was taken into federal custody and held for questioning, no one told him what he was being held for as the authorities could hold him for seventy-two hours before they would have to either charge him or let him go. Because he was held for questioning he had no right to a lawyer, and the fed's wanted as much time as possible to get answers from him before he lawyered up on them. His only clue to what they wanted from him was the question of whom he was working for, and how long he had been doing it? He refused to answer any questions whatsoever because he knew that once he started talking anything that he said could be used as evidence against him later. So badly he wanted to call Jasmine but he wasn't allowed any phone calls, funny as it seems but now he felt that if he just heard her voice that everything would be okay, even if he did feel that she betrayed him.

Chapter 29

The next morning was totally different from what Le'Roi and Colleen had experienced yesterday, the mood was different and the tension was thick in the air. There was no intimacy last night or this morning, they say that breakup sex is almost as good as make-up sex, but in this case he wouldn't find out. As she gathered her things that morning he did walk her to the car over her objections, eventually they departed to their separate ways and Le'Roi never looked back at that point, if she was looking then that was her issue to deal with. Yes he was distant and it was very obvious, he was not the type to hide his feelings very well and she knew him better than he knew himself, when he wore his emotions he wore them on his sleeve, and he really wore them ON his sleeve.

Jasmine had packed and was about to head out the door back to Columbia, Phillip still hadn't come home nor had he called. This was his normal behavior but with him being suspended from work she knew that something just wasn't quite right. In due time Phillip would eventually show with some lame excuse if any about what was going on with the investigation, and what role he played in whatever was happening. The phone rings and when she looks down at the caller ID she sees that it is Le'Roi, she quickly answers it and he hears it in her voice that she is happy to hear from him.

When are you coming back to Columbia she asks?

I'll be there tomorrow, when will you be finished in Atlanta?

Funny thing you would ask that, as I was on my way out the door to go to Columbia.

Okay, I guess then that I'll see you tomorrow.

Le'Roi, when you do get here I really need to sit down and talk to you about some things that I think are really important.

You can't tell me now?

No, this is not a good time as I want to see you face to face before I start talking, but I will tell you that Phillip has been put on administrative leave pending the outcome of an investigation of some sort and I am not being allowed back into my office until this is over.

What he screamed! What's going on?

I'm not sure she responded

Have you asked Phillip?

I haven't seen Phillip nor heard from him since he left yesterday morning. I've tried calling him on his phone but he doesn't answer and he hasn't returned my calls.

Wow, I wonder what's happening.

Another thing, Tom was found dead in his house, something about a burglary and he was killed in the process. Do you know if he and Phillip had something going on?

Jasmine I have no clue as to what is happening, look, let's finish this tomorrow when I get back.

Okay, I will call you and let you know where to meet me as we have to do this in private.

Alright, but you be careful driving back to Columbia.

And you do the same. Le'Roi?

Yes?

I really do miss you.

Same here, see you tomorrow.

Here it was he was sounding so distant again, his usual manner would be to say something along the lines of I miss you too or I miss you more, now it was reduced to a simple same here. What was going on and would he ever tell her? Jasmine didn't know but she was determined to find out. Did Phillip threaten him? If he did then she knew she had to smooth things over but how could he know about their relationship? She had to find out what Phillip knew and how much he knew about them, damn, this is getting deep. For once she realized what Le'Roi was talking about when he said Phillip would care if he found out she was sleeping with someone else, this was probably his reason for the questions he asked her. She would drive to Columbia and set things into motion for her meeting with Le'Roi, as she had to know what was happening.

Phillip's night in jail was filled with interruptions, as it seemed that as soon as he would try to fall asleep someone would come in and start questioning him again. They took turns fucking with him so that they wouldn't get tired but wanted to wear him down; he knew this so whatever they threw at him didn't work. Besides he knew that he had a heavy price to pay if he did talk and his business associates found out, hell they probably already knew about this, but that situation was one that he would deal with when he was released. Right now his sole focus was on not answering any questions until he could get a lawyer, seventy-two hours seemed like a lifetime away. Of course he didn't have a watch and the room he was in had no clock or windows so he had no concept of what time of day it was, he could only guess as to how long he had been there, wherever the hell he was.

When Jasmine arrived in Columbia, as soon as she entered the building people looked at her differently. Some were whispering and nodding in her direction, seems like word is already out she thought to herself. Of course it didn't matter what the truth was because right now the rumor mill was very strong and people have a tendency to believe the first thing that they hear, no matter what the truth may be. She was met in the hall by the secretary who informed her that the vice president wanted to see her, now what she said to herself.

She went to his office and he told her to close the door behind her and have a seat. Jasmine I'm sure by now you know that there are a lot of rumors floating around as to what's going on with Phillip he said.

Yes sir I do.

I know this makes you uncomfortable and I am not here to pass judgment, so in the interest of the company and yourself I am taking you off the reorganization team until this matter is resolved.

But sir, why are you doing this she asked.

Let me finish please, I need someone that is totally focused and not distracted by outside issues, so until this is cleared up I want you as an advisor and not the lead in the financial department. Those responsibilities will be handed by someone else and your position is strictly as an advisor.

Sir don't you think that will give the impression that I am somehow involved with what's going on?

People are going to think what they believe no matter what I do, but in the best interest of the company this is my decision. I have already cleared this with the legal department and you will still draw your salary and benefits. You will only be given work assigned by me and you will report to no one but me, do you understand?

Yes sir, but?

No buts Jasmine, do you understand?

Yes sir I do.

I realize you may be uncomfortable with my decision so I want you to take a couple of days off to take care of some personal matters, or simply think about what's going on. Take a trip or do something, just get yourself together and then come back and see me.

Am I going to be terminated?

No, you're just being reassigned as my financial department advisor. Do you have any more questions?

No sir.

Well then, I'll see you in a couple of days.

Jasmine walks out of his office and stares straight ahead when she leaves the building as she didn't want to look at anyone, the walk out the building seemed like the longest one in her life. She wanted to cry but she dare not do it in front of them, as she would appear weak. She could feel the eyes staring at her, piercing her very soul. A part of her wanted to scream out what the hell are you looking at, but like the professional she was she just kept walking.

When she entered her car she drove off and when she was away from the building she pulled over and started crying her eyes out, how could this be happening to her? What has Phillip gotten himself into, as now people thought that she was embroiled in whatever it was and she had no idea what it was. After a couple of minutes she composed herself and drove to the place they rented while in Columbia, she figured that she had best set things in motion for her and Le'Roi to talk when he arrived. She was hungry but had no appetite; she sat on the couch and just let her mind wander about the events that have unfolded in the past two days.

Le'Roi wanted to know what was going on and if anyone in Maryland had heard anything but he didn't want to ask because it wasn't his nature to get involved in other people's business, but he also didn't want anyone to question his inquiring about the situation. The best thing for him to do was wait until tomorrow when he would meet with Jasmine and they would talk and try to figure things out. What really surprised him was that although he had been distant with Jasmine lately, he still felt a yearning in his loins to be with her again, but in his mind he knew that for his own sanity he had to let her go. It hurt him to think about it but deep inside his heart he knew that was the best thing for the both of them.

Phillip was still holding tough on the outside, but inside he was weakening. He didn't know how much longer he could hold out, even his bathroom breaks were interrupted and with so little sleep his spirit was breaking. Still, he was determined to hold out as long as possible, thinking to himself that soon he would be able to get a lawyer and have the taste of freedom once again. Once he was able to be out he could begin the work of putting this thing to rest. Just hold on a little longer he kept telling himself, just a little while longer and it will all be over.

The next day Le'Roi was headed back to Columbia when he figured he would call Jasmine to tell her he was on his way. He wanted to call her last night but didn't, as he didn't want to start a conversation about what was going on and get all wrapped up in the situation but couldn't finish it. Besides, he did a lot of soul searching last night and figured that the reason he was so unfortunate with women was because he was perhaps expecting more than they were willing to give. His assuming that he and Colleen could be a couple proved that point. He did enjoy his time with Jasmine but he didn't want a relationship where he had to constantly sneak around. In the end he decided that he would rather have Jasmine in the current situation than not at all. He didn't know when it happened, but she had worked herself into his heart and he just found it hard to let her go completely, even if he and Colleen had gotten together Jasmine was always somewhere in the back of his mind. His dials the number and Jasmine answers the phone almost immediately when it rang, hi baby she says.

Well hello there, you sound good and chipper he replied.

Yes and you sound better as well, had a good night sleep?

Yeah, something like that.

Le'Roi I want you to meet me someplace when you get in if you don't mind?

No problem, I'll go home and shower and then meet you.

I was hoping that you could come straight to the place, because I really do want to see you and talk to you.

Le'Roi hears the words she has spoken and his mind instantly goes back to the last time they shared intimacy, almost immediately his manhood starts to rise. His thoughts are interrupted when he hears her ask "are you there"?

Yes I am still here.

Okay, you got quiet on me for a moment and I thought I lost the call.

Nope, I am still here he replies.

So are you going to meet me?

Yes, I will meet you when I get there, just let me know the place. When do you expect to be here?

Well since I am just leaving I should be there in about six hours or so, maybe faster depending on traffic.

Okay, I will call you back in a couple of hours with the location.

Alright, I guess I will talk to you then. Oh Jasmine, have you heard from Phillip yet?

No, I haven't heard anything at all. I don't know if anything is wrong or if he is just out on another one of his whore dates. Eventually he will come calling back soon, so I'm not going to worry about it.

Okay then, I will wait for your call.

Be careful and drive safely, later.

Later babe.

Chapter 30

Jasmine sets about putting things together for Le'Roi and their meeting, she calls and gets a room at the Charity Inn that she will pay for when she arrives. He definitely sounded different today than he did yesterday she thought, but she also knew that this would be perhaps the final time that they would be together intimately. Not sure what was really going on with Phillip, Jasmine wanted to make sure that she was there for him as the public image meant a lot to him and also to the company. She started making a list of the things that she needed to bring with her, her hygiene kit, some sexy lingerie, a bottle of wine, and more importantly, the papers. She wanted to make sure that everything was in place when Le'Roi arrived so that when he did he could relax and unwind before they started talking business. She definitely didn't forget to stop by the store and pick up some protection and lubricant, she had a plan in store for Le'Roi and since this may be the last time they could be together she wanted to fulfill a fantasy for the both of them.

As the day progresses, Phillip is finally at the point where the agents leave him alone and he is allowed to get a few hours of sleep. Of course this was also a part of their plan to keep him awake and stressed until the point where they would let him sleep for a few hours, give him a decent meal rather than the stale bologna and cheese sandwiches, all in the hopes that he would begin to cooperate and tell them what they wanted to know. Phillip is so tired that he doesn't even dream, he sits in a chair and lays his head on the table and although it is uncomfortable, he doesn't care. He is sleeping peacefully when suddenly a kick of the chair wakes him up, it seems like he just went to sleep but he has no way to tell as there is not a clock in the room and they took his watch.

Okay Phillip, you have slept for about four hours now the agent said, and I suspect that you are hungry, am I correct? Phillip just looks at the agent, not wanting to show that he was starving, for in his mind he would appear weak if he did answer. No problem, we have you a meal coming. Phillip just looked at the agent as he figured that it was nothing more than the same old stale sandwiches they had been serving before. There was a knock at the door and when opened another agent came in bearing a tray, on it was a plate with a steak, a baked potato, and a side salad. Phillip begins to salivate and tried to maintain his composure but it was obvious to everyone that he was hungry and ready to eat, maybe perhaps he was even ready to start talking.

The tray is placed in front of him and he just stares at it, go ahead, you can eat it the agent said, it's not poisoned or anything. Phillip leans forward and the smell of the meat causes his stomach to hurt, hunger pangs can be a mother sometimes. His silverware is plastic of course but he didn't care, hell he would eat with his hands if it came down to it. He starts slowly with a piece of the baked potato, never taking his eyes off the agent. Oh I forgot, you need something to drink, what would you like? Phillip doesn't respond to the question. Okay, would a soda be to your satisfaction? Phillip nods his head; this is the first time he has given any cooperation to the agents. A few minutes later an agent shows up with a can of soda, Phillip didn't care what kind it was, he just wanted something to drink. They also brought in a small bottle of water for him.

The agent sat and watched as Phillip who started eating slowly, progressed to the point where he was devouring his food. The agent never said a word as he simply watched Phillip eat like a starving animal. What would you like to tell us the agent asks? Phillip doesn't say anything, he just continues to eat. I asked you a question Phillip, is there anything that you would like to tell us? Phillip again ignores the agent and continues to eat.

Suddenly the agent knocks the food off the table and onto the floor, Phillip looks at him and then at the food that is lying nearby, then back to the agent. When I ask you a question I expect an answer, we have treated you well, fed you well and this is how you repay us! You don't deserve to eat like a decent human being; in fact your meal is over. The agent waves and another man enters the room, Phillip suddenly dives to the floor for the meat laying beside him and begins to stuff it into his mouth, the agent grabs him and tells him to spit it out, Phillip keeps chewing when suddenly the agent punches him in his stomach.

The loss of air from the punch causes Phillip to stop chewing and try to breathe, spit it out, spit it out the agent yells to Phillip. Phillip is trying to hold onto the food that is in his mouth when the agent punches him again in the stomach, this time a little harder than the last time. Phillip quickly spits the food out of his mouth and gasp for air, but this time the force of the punch is so strong that he throws up all of the food he has eaten. Now, when you are ready to play ball with us we won't do this to you, do you understand the agent said? Phillip was still wheezing trying to catch his breath, but did a little nod to acknowledge the agent's question. He now realized that his world would never be the same, before he was the big man on campus and now he was just another person being abused by the man, funny how quickly one's fall from grace can be.

Le'Roi has run into a minor traffic stall, his mind not really on anything at the moment, just wanting to get to Columbia. The more he thought about it the more he wanted Jasmine, so what if he had been with Colleen yesterday; his dick was semi-hard and throbbing at the thought of seeing Jasmine and her perky nipples begging him to suck them. Since traffic was so slow, Le'Roi decided to get off at the next exit ramp and grab something quick to eat; it would be at the drive-thru as he didn't want to lose any time getting back to Columbia. After he got his food he headed back to the interstate, traffic was still a bit slow but it was moving a little bit faster, he was about to take a drink of his soda when the car beside him just came over into his lane and cut him off. To avoid the accident Le'Roi had to jerk the wheel and his soda spilled all over his clothes, he was cussing up a storm but the damage had already been done. His mind came off the driving incident when the phone rang and he saw it was Jasmine.

Hello?

Hey baby, I got us a room at the Charity Inn.

Why there he asked?

Because what I want to discuss with you is private and we needed someplace private to go to.

We could have met someplace different he replied. He didn't know why he was saying these things as they just seem to come to mind.

Like where? Your place? My place? Too much of a chance of someone seeing us so I felt this was safer.

For once now she was using her head he thought, sometimes later is better than not at all. I understand he said, what room?

Well as you would say, the number of the day is 110.

His mind thought back to the first time they went there in room 110, okay, whenever I get out of this mess I will be there.

Alright then, I guess I will see you there.

Okay, later babe.

Muuauh, that's a kiss from me to you she responded.

And I got it, all of it he said with laughter before hanging up the phone.

Jasmine had everything set up and in place, still her mind went back to Phillip and where the hell he was. She hated him for tormenting her like this, but she also liked the fact that with him being away she could have one more night with Le'Roi before she broke it off with him. Le'Roi's mind was on nothing more than getting back to Columbia and out of that damn traffic, he couldn't wait to get there and the first thing he would do would be to take a shower. The spilled soda on his body made him feel sticky and he didn't like that, so before they would talk about anything he had to take a shower and change his clothes.

Later that day when Le'Roi neared the Charity Inn he called Jasmine to let her know that he was nearby, although Phillip was in Atlanta, he was still cautious and wanted to make sure he wasn't being watched. She answered and told him that she would leave the door cracked so that he could come straight into the room. Le'Roi parks the car and scans the area as always, he didn't have a reason to; he just wanted to be sure.

When he enters the room Jasmine immediately comes over to him and hugs him tightly, he hugs her in return but the only thing on his mind right now is a shower as he is sticky from the soda that was spilled on him and the sweat from driving. She leans her head back and kisses him passionately on the lips; her kiss does something to him as now he returns her kiss with more passion than what she gave to him. His manhood starts to rise and he pushes himself closer to her, while reaching around with his hands and grabbing her butt to pull her closer to him. She feels the bulge in his pants pressing against her and she is ready for him, her juices have been flowing for the past hour as she knew for sure that she was about to get some relief. Yes she could have used her hands or a toy, but there was nothing like the sensation of having a nice hard dick stuck up inside your dripping wet pussy. Just thinking about it caused her to moan and grab him tighter.

Le'Roi sees where this is about to go and breaks the passionate kiss they just shared, yes his dick is hard but he wants to shower before he does anything else. Jasmine doesn't like it as she wants him now and doesn't care how he smells, but he needs a shower and that is what he is going to get. She watches him as he undresses, first his shirt followed by his pants. Jasmine loved watching him in his underwear, the briefs he wore couldn't hide the fact that he was excited, if anything they kept him confined when his dick wanted to be set free. Le'Roi takes off his tee shirt and socks, right now he is standing before her with nothing on but his drawers, the bulge in them makes her mouth water as she is ready to suck some dick and have him deep inside of her.

Le'Roi takes his soap and goes into the shower, a nice hot shower would make him feel much better. When he went into the bathroom Jasmine cleared everything off the bed and placed the condoms on the table next to the side of the bed that Le'Roi would be laying, he didn't know it but she was also getting undressed and she was going to join him in the shower. The water felt good as it hit Le'Roi's body, though the drive was only about seven hours, it seemed like a long time and he couldn't wait to get out of the car and into the shower. He would have preferred to go to his own place and shower but since Jasmine was so insistent, he didn't see the need to argue, maybe she really did want him here. That didn't matter as he still felt the urge for excitement in his lions and he wanted to get up inside of her as soon as he was finished with the shower.

Le'Roi was captivated with his own thoughts and didn't even notice that Jasmine had entered the bathroom; he was startled when she pulled back the curtain and entered the shower. He turned to look at her and was about to say something when she put her fingers to his lips to quiet him. He turned back around and stared straight ahead when he felt the heat of her body pressing against his as her hands came around the front of his body and rubbed his chest. The feel of her hands gliding across the water and rubbing his nipples caused his dick to become fully erect. He closed his eyes and just enjoyed the sensation when her hands moved down across his belly and stopped at his throbbing penis, she takes him in both of her hands and squeezes his member, when she releases him he becomes even harder.

She releases her grip and takes the soap off the shower caddy and lathers her hands, then moves it back down to his member which is so hard it could poke a hole in the wall. Jasmine kisses him on his back and slowly begins to stroke his member with her right hand while her left hand rubs his chest. After stroking him slowly for awhile she moves her hand down to his balls and gently rubs them, the slipperiness of the soap makes it easy for her hands to move all over his body. He didn't tell her this, but her touch had caused him to become very aroused, so much to the point that he thought he would explode at any moment.

He turns around to face her before he blew his load in the shower, his mouth moves to hers and their tongues touch each other. Each has missed the touch and passion of the other and while they didn't know it, they both had subconsciously compared their other lovers to each other; both realizing that the person they were with did not provide the same passion and intensity as the one they desired. Yes they were good together, but would that be enough to sustain them was his thought, while she was wavering on telling him it was over. She wanted to and needed to but the way he made her feel so alive was an experience like none she ever had before.

Le'Roi moves his mouth down to her breasts, her nipples are fully swollen and he likes the way they feel in his mouth. His tongue would flicker across them and circle the peaks, he loved doing that and it brought her so much excitement. His hand went down below to her crouch and he could feel that her juices were flowing; it wasn't the water as she was so slippery that he knew she was ready for him. He was consumed with his own quest for fulfillment when he suddenly raised his head and begins gulping down air, apparently he didn't think about the shower and when the water rushed over his face he just panicked.

Okay that's enough; let's take this into the next room she said. Le'Roi exited the shower and Jasmine stayed in to clean herself up. Le'Roi saw that she had already prepared the bed and the fact that she even brought condoms, guess there's no need to figure what's on her mind he thought. He got in bed and waited for her to finish her shower when he noticed a package sitting by the television, it was unlikely that she had brought work with her but he wasn't going to worry about that right now.

She came into the room with the towel about her body, the look in her eyes told him that she was horny and wanted him now. She takes a chair and sets it next to the bed, sit here she commanded. Puzzled but willing to play along, he gets out of bed and sits in the chair. Jasmine gets down on her knees and puts him inside of her mouth, he loves the warm sensation and reaches down to squeeze her breasts under the towel she is still wearing. She pulls back and looks at him and says, not yet. She pushes him toward the back of the chair and resumes performing fellatio on him, and then she stands up and straddles him, slowly inserting his manhood inside her wet box.

Le'Roi likes this even more and the intensity builds up inside of him and he begins to move to meet her when she again stops him, let me do this she said. Le'Roi looks at her, smiles, then sits back to enjoy the ride. He wants to move and meet her bounces but he wanted to let her do what it was she wanted to do. Jasmine stops, climbs off him and puts him back into her mouth, licking and sucking his tool as if it were a piece of candy. She then stands up, grabs a condom, and removes the towel from her body, she leans forward and kisses him passionately while climbing back on top of him without breaking the kiss.

They each work themselves into a rhythm in the chair, her bouncing up and down on him and he has his hands on her hips helping her along. He reaches around and feels that her backside is wet so he slips a finger inside her ass, initially she stops and he thinks he is hurting her. Does this hurt? No, it feels kind of good. Want me to stop? No, but don't get crazy either she says with a small laugh. The sensation that she is having from his finger is one that she has never experienced before, she knew about anal sex but no one has ever performed it with her. One thing that she liked about Le'Roi was his sensitivity and gentleness; he was always concerned about hurting her whereas other guys just didn't care. The insertion of his finger in her ass while his dick is in her pussy makes her have an orgasm, as she grabs the chair and her body trembles on top of his.

They continue on a bit more before moving to the bed, Le'Roi is in her and pushing himself very deep inside her when she looks at him and says "let's do anal". Le'Roi keeps going as he really didn't hear what she said, he heard what he thought she said but dismissed it because it just couldn't be true. Did you hear me she asked? What did you say? I said let's do anal. At his point Le'Roi stops and looks her in the eyes, there is a glow about her as she seems excited. Are you sure about this? Yeah she said with eagerness in her voice. Le'Roi comes out of her and leans back, okay, but if it starts to hurt to the point where it is unbearable tell me and I will stop. Oh don't worry, I will definitely tell you she said as she reached into the night stand drawer and took out the lubrication gel.

Damn, she came prepared for everything he thought to himself. Okay, how do you want me she asked? Lay on your side. Wait, first tell me what you are going to do so that I can know what to expect. I'll have you lay on your side and I'll then grab some lubrication and slide my finger into your butt while sucking your breasts. My finger will slowly move in and out of you before I increase the speed. Then I'll put another finger in and wiggle it to help relax the muscle. I'll lubricate myself and slowly enter your ass while spreading your cheek with my free hand. I'll gently slide in and out and suck your breasts to help you to relax, only going as far as you can tolerate. I'll stroke it slowly, then faster while playing with your clit. I'll put my finger in your box as I stroke in and out of your butt hole.

Hopefully you will begin to relax and realize that you actually enjoy the anal sex and slowly begin moving in the same rhythm as I do. You move further back to take it deeper as I continue to stroke you and rub your swollen clit, then it happens. You feel the passion building inside you and then explode with a force you have never experienced before. The orgasm is so intense that you forget about where I am inside of you and buck against my hips moving my dick further into your ass. Your excitement causes me to unload my hot cum all over your body. The experience was something we both enjoyed and treasured.

Hearing him describe this has caused a stir within her, as her pussy becomes soaking wet from the thought of his hands all over her body and his manhood being in her holes. She didn't understand why she felt that way, especially about the anal sex part, but it seems as though he has aroused a desire within her that Phillip once did many years ago. During the entire time he was explaining to her what he was going to do his fingers were playing in her ass. Initially when he put two fingers in he had to back off because it caused her some discomfort, but soon he was able to do it but not as rough or as far as he did with one finger.

Okay, I am ready but if you hurt me we will stop. I won't hurt you Jasmine, and I will be gentle. That's the only reason you are the one doing this she replied. As he told her before, he had her lay on her side and he was slow in his approach. The beginning was a bit uncomfortable for Jasmine, she didn't know if the pain was that intense or was it exaggerated based on her fears. Eventually she was able to relax and somewhat enjoy it until the times when he tried to put all of himself inside of her. She was able to relax and enjoy the experience with him, he was special to her and no man had ever been in her ass before, and as far as she was concerned Le'Roi would be the only man that would ever go back there. Le'Roi did cum and sprays his load on her body, while she was excited from the anal sex, she didn't achieve an orgasm like he predicted. It didn't matter to her, she was content with what they just shared and hoped that he saw how special he was to her by what she did.

They both lay down next to each other when Jasmine heard a beep on her phone, she grabbed it thinking it was Phillip but the caller I.D. showed the company number. She thought about calling back but decided not to as she wanted to enjoy the moment with Le'Roi, it was a shame that she had to break it off with him, but deep down inside she knew that it was the right thing to do. The two of them shortly fall asleep from the peacefulness that surrounded them.

Chapter 31

About an hour later he wakes up and looks at her sleeping, she was a beautiful sight to see. He was into his own thoughts when she said "why are you looking at me?" How did you know? I could sense it and besides, I knew you were awake because you stopped snoring. I'm sorry, guess I was a bit tired. That's cool; we might as well get up. Yes, I am curious to know what it is you wanted to tell me.

Le'Roi gets up and goes into the bathroom and closes the door behind him, Jasmine sits up in the bed and turns on the television and starts flipping through the channels. Le'Roi flushes the toilet when he hears Jasmine scream, he rushes out in the room and she has her mouth open and pointing at the television. Le'Roi sees it is Phillip in hand cuffs being escorted out of a courtroom and presumably headed back to jail. Jasmine grabs her phone and calls the company to speak to the vice president, he doesn't want to discuss the issue on the phone but Jasmine's persistence and screaming makes him comply.

She finds out that Phillip is being held in the county lockup in South Carolina and was charged with money laundering and carrying a concealed weapon without a permit. Phillip was in the custody of the federal agents and moved from Atlanta, but a plea deal worked out provided that he be placed in a state run institution where the restrictions are not as harsh as the federal institutions, this was done by Phillip's willingness to cooperate and be afforded protection. Jasmine quickly showers and gets dressed before rushing out the door headed to the jail to see Phillip, Le'Roi doesn't say a word as what do you really say at a time like that. Besides, the look on her face told him that she didn't want to hear a word from anybody, including him.

Jasmine arrives at the county jail and though it is not the normal visiting day for family and friends, Jasmine was given a special provision to see Phillip that was arranged through negotiation with the company. It was a one time provision since Phillip had been detained and she had not heard from him. She is searched and escorted to a room where she sees a booth with a chair, on the other side was another chair and a glass wall separated both sides. There was a telephone that was used for talking to the other party. She waits for what seems like an hour when Phillip finally arrives, she jumps up but he moves his hands to tell her to sit down.

The guard that escorted him to the room leaves and Phillip picks up the telephone, motioning for her to do the same. Be careful what you say because we are being recorded he tells her, she nods. They both just stare at each other when Phillip asks her how she was doing. Fine? What's going on here she asks?

You know damn well what's going on he yells?

Shocked at his demeanor, she replies what do you mean?

How could you do this to me? After all I have done for you, for us, your mother? I don't understand.

Jasmine lowers her head as she comes to the realization that Phillip knows about her affair with Le'Roi. I'm sorry Phillip.

Of all the people around me I never expected it to be you as the one that would betray me.

It was just something that happened and one thing led to another and . . .

Don't feed me that bullshit, you knew damn well what you were doing he screamed at her. At this point the guard comes in and looks at Phillip with a scowl that says quiet it down, so Phillip tries to calm himself.

You're right, I really have no excuse but sometimes the way you treated me and made me feel I just . . .

Phillip cuts her off and says, I should have known better than to trust a bitch. Tears begin to stream down Jasmine's face; she knew she was wrong for what she did, but she didn't understand what her affair had to do with Phillip being in jail.

I know you are upset with me, but I have broken off the relationship with him and I want us to work on our marriage.

Stunned, Phillip looks at her with a puzzled look and says, "what relationship"?

The one between me and Le'Roi she answers.

You had a relationship with Le'Roi?

Isn't that what you are talking about she responded.

No, I'm talking about the Zylander Company that you kept inquiring about.

Now she is confused, what about Zylander?

You mean to tell me you fucked Le'Roi?

Why are you in here she asks?

You fucked Le'Roi, that motherfucker.

The guard comes in and says, time's up. Phillip looks at Jasmine and says, get the fuck out of my life you stupid bitch, slams the phone down, and walks away with the guard.

Jasmine leaves and decides to stop by the house before she heads back to the hotel, she had completely forgotten about Le'Roi and when she arrived home he would be even further off her mind. Her house was filled with agents in the yard, because Phillip was charged with money laundering, all of his assets were frozen or taken into possession by the federal authorities until it could be determined what was not bought with the illegal proceeds. Then those possessions would be released to the family, in this case it was Jasmine. She was not allowed into the house to retrieve anything; she could only go in when things were resolved.

Her cell phone rings and she doesn't want to answer it but does so anyway, it was her mother. The federal agents had seized the house her mother was in as well, with her mother upset and with no place to go Jasmine told her she would wire her some money so that she could live in a hotel for a few days until she could sort this whole thing out. Then it occurred to Jasmine, why had no one questioned her about what was going on? Not that she wanted to volunteer any information but why was she left alone?

She departs the area and heads to an ATM machine and withdraws some money, she stops by a convenience store and wires it to her mother. While there she picks up a few items and then heads back to the hotel, when she enters she sees that Le'Roi is still there and he has been reading through the papers that they were supposed to talk about. Neither said anything and when the tears formed in her eyes he immediately got up and takes her in his arms to console her, she cried something fierce and he let her do it.

Reading the papers and looking at the news enabled him to piece all of the activities together, but how much of it was the truth and what was being embellished by the media? He didn't know and he didn't want to pass judgment on Phillip as many people are so quick to rush to judgment without knowing all of the facts. When Jasmine settled down they went to a restaurant, she wasn't hungry but he wanted to at least give her the opportunity to eat something.

They sat across from each other in the booth, if she wasn't going to eat then neither was he, so each just had a beverage. Jasmine told him about the encounter with Phillip in the jail and how he thought that she had something to do with his being arrested. She also told him that she told Phillip about the affair when she realized he didn't know what was going on. Jasmine and Phillip each assumed the other person knew what they were doing, but in the end neither had a clue until the visit in the jail. Le'Roi then told her what he thought was true from the papers he saw in the hotel and why he thought Phillip was arrested.

When they left the restaurant they stopped by the store, although Phillip was mad with her she was willing to be there for him in court, so she bought some clothes to take back to the hotel. Le'Roi offered her the opportunity to stay in his guest bedroom at the house but she thought better of it, as with all the attention on Phillip you didn't know who may be watching her and the last thing she wanted to do was get Le'Roi involved in their situation. Le'Roi took Jasmine back to the hotel and out of respect for her; he then departed to his own residence. There was a lot of media coverage surrounding the arrest of Phillip, every channel that Le'Roi turned to had someone speaking on the case, finally he turned the television off and tried to sleep, but his mind was on Jasmine and how when she really needed someone, he couldn't help her.

The next day Jasmine was in court for Phillips arraignment, when he entered the courtroom and saw her, he quickly turned his head as if he didn't see her, this hurt her feelings but she was going to be there for him whether he wanted her there or not. Phillip was remanded to the court as he was considered a flight risk; with his assets tried up he couldn't afford a high profile lawyer. The court was going to make a determination in two weeks on what assets were to remain seized and what could be released. Phillip left the courtroom without even looking Jasmine's way; he should have taken the look because tomorrow is not promised to anyone.

Jasmine left the courtroom and after getting pass the mob of media that hounded her for a statement, she set out to get her affairs in order, she needed to prove what assets she had that had nothing to do with the current situation. She was allowed escorted access into the house for the purpose of gathering her papers, she then hired a lawyer to fight her cause, it wasn't so much what she wanted, but the house that her mother lived in and the one in Atlanta was her concern.

Later that night Phillip went to take a shower, usually there was someone there but this time the place was empty and he enjoyed his alone time. While he was accustomed to being the big man, in here he was just another person and if not careful, he could end up somebody's bitch. Two guys came in and started showering; he didn't make eye contact with them because in prison that was something you just didn't do. Another came in and Phillip still had no reason to suspect anything, maybe he should have wished his intuition was on because he was in for a very big surprise.

Suddenly two more guys came in and Phillip became nervous, you scared homey one guy asked? Naw man. Well maybe you should be, bitch! Suddenly a flurry of fist and feet begin kicking and beating the shit out of Phillip, the punches were so many that he didn't know where they were coming from. Finally they stopped beating him and he was held down to the floor with his hands behind his back. In walked someone else but Phillip's vision was so blurred from the beating that he couldn't make out who it was, is this him he asked? Yeah, this is the motherfucker. Okay, have your fun.

Phillip was turned over onto his stomach and he knew what was coming next, no, please he screamed. The men just laughed at him, now you want to beg one said. He was held down so tightly that he couldn't move and whenever he did resist a bit too much a punch or two to the face usually settled him down. His legs were forced apart and his asshole was entered by one of the gang that held him in the shower, how do you like it now bitch? Phillip fought to get away and tried to scream his lungs out; he felt that his asshole was being ripped apart from the ferocious fucking he was taking. When the first one was done the next took over, this continued until all of the men had their turn using him as their bitch.

The man who came in last walked over and said to him, tell everyone, your ass belongs to me, got it bitch! By the way, that was for my cousin he said right before he kicked Phillip in the gut. Phillip lay on the floor as the men left the shower area, his ass raw from the rape he had just endured. His mind thought about the things he had done to other people without any regard for them as a person, now he was reaping back what he had given out. He knew that he needed to pay those fuckers back once he got out, but that was for later as he first had to survive being here. He should have been paying attention but he wasn't, as he was in his own world about the things he had done and would do, but even if he had been paying attention his efforts would not have amounted to anything.

Suddenly he felt a knee in his back and someone grabbing his head and pulling it back, he was not going to be raped again he told himself even though he was powerless to do anything. A face leaned forward and whispered in his ear, we always clean up our mess. Fear suddenly struck Phillip like none he had experienced; he felt an initial pain on his neck followed by a warm sensation. When his head was let go he realized that he was bleeding, he got up and tried to talk but his throat had been slit from ear to ear. He frantically tried to call for help as he saw the life spurt from his body. He begins feeling tired and falls down; he sits up against the wall while his mind flashes to a variety of scenes in his life. His last thought was of Jasmine and how he wished he could see her right now and hold her in his arms. He's getting sleepy but tries to fight and stay awake, he slumps over and thinks "what about Jasmine, what about Jasmine?"

Phillip's death in prison shocked everyone, especially Jasmine as even though they had rough times, she didn't want anything to happen to him, especially something like that. The funeral held was a small one with family and very close friends, out of respect for Jasmine Le'Roi didn't go, even though she had not asked him to stay away.

Jasmine was able to prove that a lot of the assets in question were purchased before the Zylander money laundering scheme developed. Her mother was able to move back into her house and Jasmine back into hers. The children were given a large amount of money from the insurance proceeds, and Jasmine as the beneficiary on all the other property, inherited everything.

Phillip was laundering the money for a drug cartel and used the Zylander Company as his cover, money was wired to off shore accounts and then Phillip would send the money back as a payment from the phony company. His operation had been ongoing for almost three years; he tried to do it alone but needed some help. He recruited the others by not only paying them money, but also by holding some of their activities over their heads, the parties were not just for pleasure, but they also served a business purpose. The money in the off-shore accounts were seized by the government, but the good thing was that Jasmine, and Phillip's two children were in no financial strain.

Jasmine and Le'Roi never became intimate after that last night together; it was sort of an unspoken agreement between the two of them. He was there for her during the entire process of the funeral and trial, his role was to help her from the background and not the front. They talked but as time went on they spoke less to each other, not sure if the other needed space, they just didn't talk. Eventually Jasmine left her position at the company and no one ever suspected that the two of them had anything going on.

Later Jasmine sold the house in Atlanta and moved on, no one was really sure where she went, while they didn't talk that much when all of this first started, there was definitely no communications between them now. Le'Roi would often wonder how she was doing and what she was doing, but he was also hurt that she didn't say goodbye. Maybe that was the way she wanted it, or perhaps her leaving may have been too much for her to handle if she saw him. Often times his mind would go back to the final time they were together, and he realized just how special she thought he was by giving of herself that day. His thoughts were on a lot of things about her, as he felt that she was the complete woman in every aspect of the word. He had never met a woman like her and figured he never would again in his lifetime.

Phillip all the while thought it was Jasmine who had turned him in for the money laundering scheme, when in fact it was James. All of the records of the illegal transactions were erased, but Tom made a copy of them as a backup for himself. Tom had ideas of taking over the team from Phillip and once during a drunken conversation, he let James in on what he was doing. James took the paperwork and copied it for himself; it was also he who gave the information to Jasmine. When James would visit her office he would take the tape from that day and replace it with an older one that had no incriminating information. No one knew it, but he had dodged a bullet the day Phillip asked to see the tapes, because had he listened to them he might have discovered that they were just copies of earlier conversations. Coleman's murder was just a random act of violence during a robbery attempt when he tried to fight back.

James took his information to the executive director after Phillip essentially embarrassed him by questioning his loyalty; he was given immunity from prosecution if he could prove that the money laundering took place. In exchange for his cooperation he would be given protective custody and the company would not be faced with a public scandal, as their name would be kept out of the news. Unknowing to James or anyone else, he would also help to expose a mole inside the agency, the agent that killed Tom was cornered and committed suicide rather than be charged and face the "organization" he worked for, because he had seen their methods of torture and he would rather die than be handed over to them. In the end of things the old adage holds true, keeps your friends close, and your enemies closer, but sometimes you need to flip it around.

The young lady from the restaurant never got to witness just how badly Phillip was treated during his "lesson" in prison, but it was satisfaction enough knowing that he was given worse than what he did to her.

The initial plan was to just kill Phillip, but a deal worked out between inmates made sure that Phillip would get his just desserts before his "client" took care of their business.

Le'Roi eventually left the company and moved on, his thoughts of his childhood and past memories now included Jasmine. He never sought the help of a mental specialist, so he still had to contend with his thoughts waking him up at night. One thing he realized was while he was with Jasmine, the thoughts subsided, and now they were back as if they knew she had left. Maybe he would see her again one day, he wasn't sure, but destiny has a way of working things out, at least that is what he had hoped for.

The End

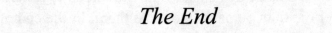

Their meeting was one that was filled with emotion and excitement, it had been a couple of years since they were together and though they knew each other, this moment seemed a bit awkward. They greet and it seems as if they've never left each other's side, each catches the other up on things that have occurred during their absence, and both are surprised to find that the other is not with anyone. After lunch they head back to his place to continue their conversation and reestablished friendship. As the day progresses she figures it is best that she departs, she didn't want to give the wrong impression by staying so long and as she gets up to leave he takes her in his arms and plants a kiss on her lips, slowly allowing his tongue to slide against hers. Initially she is shocked, but the feelings that she once had are now starting to resurface again, she doesn't want to continue but the feeling from his kiss and touch is so overwhelming that she allows herself to enjoy the passion that she is feeling.

He pulls her closer to him as his manhood starts to rise; she hungrily kisses him back as she feels his hands on her butt. Her juices are starting to flow and she wants to feel him inside of her again, just to see if the feeling would be the same. He breaks the kiss and moves his mouth to her breast, she helps by unbuttoning her blouse and exposing the semi hard nipple that wants to be kissed and sucked. His mouth covers her tit and his hand squeezes it like a piece of fruit. Her groin is aching to feel the hardness of his tool deep inside her; she reaches down and rubs the hardness in his pants. Funny, it appears larger now than it did the last time she remembered. She steps back and says "take off your clothes".

He smiles and removes his shirt, exposing the muscular chest that wants to hold her. He takes off his pants and now is standing there with just his underwear and socks on. The socks are next when he slowly removes his underwear, setting free the rock hard tool that wants to get inside of her juicy wetness. The look on her face is of surprise and excitement; she looks at him and says . . . .

AWWWWWWWWW

As I lay in the bed motionless, I can't believe what just happened,
My girl just took all of my energy, but I am filled with satisfaction.
Now I'm in a state of shock because she has never been one to take control,
But tonight, she was aggressive and sexually bold.
When I walked in the door she led me to the room,
Pushed me down on the bed, took our clothes off until we both were in the nude.
Kissing me all over starting from the top,
Started focusing on my midsection, making my dick head prop.
In and out of her mouth, going up and down my shaft,
Slapping it on her chin until I could no longer last.
She took some of it and spread the rest on her face,
And said "baby that was good, I love the way you taste".
Now it's my turn, I couldn't wait to wrap her legs around my neck,
As I went to turn her over, she pushed me down and said "I'm not done with you yet".
She puts her tongue on my sack and started again to lick and suck my dick,
I know I just came, but she got me back hard like a brick.
She knows I can't resist the urge to take control,
So she pulled out the handcuffs and locked me to the bed post.
Now she's riding and I can tell by the way her body is starting to shake,
That she was cumming, but she still kept moving her body like a snake.
She's going up and down, backwards, slow then fast,
Making me wish I could rip off these handcuffs so I could smack that ass.

Now I'm about to cum, but I've never felt like this when
I'm about to unload,
My soldiers are marching faster, I'm yelling, and then I
start to explode.
Now I'm speechless, I can't move a muscle, and I don't
know what's up,
She said "any woman can make you cum, but it takes a
bitch to make you nut".
And that she did, I can't believe I let out that much cum,
She pleased me completely through and I guess that's why
I'm sprung.

Printed in the United States
98077LV00004B/310/A